W9-BXK-370

SKIES OVER SWEETWATER is a selection of:

- THE CHILDREN'S BOOK-OF-THE-MONT[...]
- THE LITERARY GUILD™
- CROSSINGS BOOK CLUB™
- THE QUALILTY PAPERBACK BOOK CLUB™

What the Reviewers are saying. . .

The story is compelling, and it sheds light on a little-known piece of [...] serve as an inspiration to anyone who dreams of doing the unconve[...]

–School Library Journal

An inspiring portrayal of America's first military-trained female pilots, [...] forgotten part of history to light and showing that men were not the only [...] during World War II.

–BookPage

Moberg has done solid research, crafting a believable story that realistically [...] known segment of history. Easy to read, a very manageable length, "Skies O[...] a great story both in and out of the classroom, perfect for the dreaming days o[...] ahead.

–The Press & Sun-Bulletin (Binghamton, NY)

My thanks to [Julia] for writing about the Women Airforce Service Pilots during [...]

–Laura Bush, First Lady of the United States of America

Julia Moberg's "Skies Over Sweetwater" is an extraordinary tale of friendship, loyal[...] ism a coming-of-age story about the serendipity that occurs when we reach deep dow[...] the courage to follow our dreams. This is an exciting novel and Moberg's writing is re[...] of Harper Lee's tender, yet powerful narration in "To Kill a Mockingbird." This is an [...] cious debut from a writer with a very bright future.

–Gary Jansen, Executive Editor, Quality Paperback Book Club

I am delighted to offer "Skies Over Sweetwater" in the **Children's Book-of-the-Month Clu**[...] It is exceptionally well written and full of adventure, putting the reader in the middle of each scene. I am watching intently for this book to become a bestseller soon.

–Desmond Campbell, Editor, Children's Book-of-the-Month-Club

"Skies Over Sweetwater" is an intriguing novel, reminds me of that movie, "A League of Their Own" A part of history I never knew of and so valuable in our library to have that part of his-tory put into such an accessible text—accessible across ages and genders too, a rare find.

–Carol McCoy, Youth Services Librarian

Skies Over Sweetwater

Library Media Center
Sarah Gibbons Middle School
20 Fisher Street
Westborough, MA 01581

A NOVEL

by

JULIA MOBERG

KEENE
PUBLISHING
Warwick, NY

F
MOB
92642

This novel is a work of fiction. Names, characters, places, and incidents (other than historical facts) either are the product of the author's imagination or are used fictitiously, and any resemblance to actual persons, living or dead, events, or locales is entirely coincidental.

P. O. Box 54
Warwick, New York 10990
www.KeeneBooks.com

Text copyright © 2008 Julia Moberg.

All rights reserved. First Edition.

Cover graphic concept by Tom Lennon. Cover image of girl with plane copyright © Dana Tynan/Corbis. Woman pilot photo copyright © Patrick Moberg (model Anna Sebestyen). Back cover author photo by Scott Totty. Final cover image, copyright © 2008 Keene Publishing.

Text set in Adobe Jenson and Numbus Script, with titles in Trajan Pro.

Published by Keene Publishing in Warwick, NY. For information on permission to reproduce, or about this and other Keene Publishing and Moo Press titles, please email info@KeeneBooks.com or write to Keene Publishing, PO Box 54, Warwick, NY 10990. To order copies of this book, visit our Web site bookstore at www.KeeneBooks.com or visit your local bookstore. Readers guides available online; bulk discount for book club groups and schools available.

LIBRARY OF CONGRESS CATALOGING IN PUBLICATION DATA
Available upon request.
ISBN: 978-0-9792371-2-6

Printed in the United States of America

on 100% Recycled Paper.

10 9 8 7 6 5 4 3 2

10/09

I dedicate this book to the
Women's Airforce Service Pilots of
WWII.

May your story continue to be told
for decades to come...

~ J.M.

ACKNOWLEDGMENTS

First and foremost, I'd like to thank Elizabeth Fisher at the Levine Greenberg agency for believing in this story from day one. Throughout each draft, your editorial feedback and support was invaluable, and I am forever grateful to your diligence and willingness to go above and beyond. Thanks also to Stephanie Rostan, Jim Levine, and Daniel Greenberg for trusting in Elizabeth's conviction that this book could find a home.

To the book's home, Keene Publishing & Moo Press: You have made my dream a reality. Thanks to my publisher, Diane Tinney, for being excited about the book and taking a chance on a first time author. To Melissa Browne, Lauren Manoy, and Mindy Kole. Thank you all for your hard work in making this book the best it could be.

To Linda Gottlieb, who introduced me to the WASP in the first place. Without you, this book would not exist.

To the real life WASP, whose stories inspired and offered me guidance throughout the writing process: Cornelia Fort, Marion Stegeman Hodgson, Betty Greene, Margaret J. Ringenberg, and Deanie Parrish.

To my parents, Catherine and David. You are the BEST parents anyone could hope for. Thank you for your never-ending support and undying love. It all started in elementary school when you helped me write my first poem for Arbor Day. And it won!

To Michael and Patrick. Each of you inspires me in your own special way. I am proud to be a sister to you both.

To Grandpa Lowell. Thank you for lending me your first name. I love you dearly.

To Sam. Thank you for the laughter, love, and encouragement. I would say that I couldn't do it without you, but your response would be, "Yes, you could." I'm just glad I don't have to.

And to all my friends and family. I am honored to have you in my life. Special thanks to Chris Wiggins for letting me pick your pilot brain. Anna Sebestyen for gracing the book cover with your gorgeous face, and Embrey Bronstad for your love and sisterhood. And, to my writer buds: Tricia, Jen, Mark, Edith, and Damian: You make living a joy.

This book was written to music from the 1940s, namely The Andrew Sisters, Bing Crosby, Nat King Cole, Dinah Shore, and The Glenn Miller Orchestra.

Once you have flown,
you will walk the earth
with your eyes turned skyward,
for there you have been,
and there you long to return.

-LEONARDO DA VINCI

Library Media Center
Sarah Gibbons Middle School
20 Fisher Street
Westborough, MA 01581

PROLOGUE
1936

Pa turned back toward the controls and started the engine up. Mom stood below on the ground, shaking her head in disapproval.

"Prepare for takeoff!" Pa shouted as the propeller began to spin and the engine rumbled, causing my heart to jump with nervous excitement. Less than a minute later, we lurched forward and began to drive along the endless stretch of grass behind our house. Rolling down the field, our speed increased and the plane zigzagged to each side, as it usually did the minute before we took off. Pa gently pulled back on the stick and I could feel the plane's wheels lift up off the ground with a jolt as we began our ascent.

As we lifted up and over the cornfields off in the distance, the wind whipped my hair in all directions and the force of gravity pushed me back against the seat as our pace increased and we gained altitude. The air in my lungs plunged to the pit of my stomach as the nose of the plane tilted up toward the clouds, and the earth below dropped farther and farther away from us.

I looked at the altimeter, just like he taught me to. We were at 13,000 feet. I could feel the plane turn to one side. We were about to do a spin. As we tilted toward the left side, I stared down at the world below us. I could see our farmhouse and the neighbor's horses. The cornfields stretched out in all directions and intricate patterns, and with the sun shining down, it looked like a giant sea of gold thread. It was the first crop of the summer.

Above us, the clouds danced all around, and I imagined what it would be like to live in a house made of clouds. And to eat clouds instead of food. They would taste like cotton candy. Or mashed potatoes.

"Thinking about the clouds again?" Pa yelled at me. I nodded. "You'll be the next Amelia Earhart, and I'll make sure of it!" I smiled. Pa always told me things like that. He loved how excited I was about flying.

"Dive, Pa. Please," I pleaded.

Dives were my favorite. I loved the way they felt. All the breath in my body would leave for a moment, and I would become a little light-headed. It was better than the roller coaster ride at the Iowa State Fair.

"Hold on tight!" Pa yelled. But instead of holding on, I raised my arms high above my head and tried to touch the clouds as they zipped by us, faster than the speed of light.

"We'll be back!" I told them.

We began to fall downward, and my heart danced. Down, down, down we went, and I allowed my eyes to close as the wind ran its spindly fingers through my hair and rippled against my eyelashes. And that's when the shaking began.

I tried to open my eyes but they wouldn't budge. Neither would either of my arms. I could feel the wind flapping against my face. It was faster and stronger than I had ever felt it before, and a thundering noise echoed in both of my ears. When I called out for Pa, I couldn't even hear my own voice.

And then everything suddenly turned to black.

CHAPTER ONE
1944

The train pulls up to the station, right on time. The conductor helps lug my trunk up the stairs and into my compartment. I sit down on the gorgeous plush red velvet bench where I will be spending the next 12 hours. I run my fingers over it, realizing how long it has been since I felt anything so wonderful.

Outside the window the Iowa sun is starting to come up all purple and orange over the horizon. I think about Mom and my sister, Charlotte, and I wonder if they are awake yet and if they've noticed I'm gone. And then I think about Pa, and it hurts, so I open my trunk and find my favorite and only book I own, *West with the Night*, by Beryl Markham. I get lost reading about her adventures flying her plane across the Atlantic. Then, without realizing it, I am asleep.

I can never sleep long because the fire always comes. When I doze off, my eyes fill up with orange and red. They burn, and someone is always screaming my name, and my head feels like it's going to explode. Right before it does, I wake up.

For a moment I am disoriented and forget where I am until the grumbling clatter of the engine jogs my memory, reminding me that I'm on the train. I shake the fire out of my head. My stomach is growling and sore with hunger, so I pull out the apple I pocketed. I am about to take a bite when I look up and become aware of a set of eyes watching me attentively.

A girl is sitting across from me. She is around eighteen, the same age as me. Her hair is a bright shade of auburn-red and her eyes are the color of ginger. She's wearing a crisp white blouse tucked into a pair of blue pants and freshly polished black and white saddle shoes. I stare at her, realizing I had never seen a girl wearing pants before. Mom would be appalled.

"Got any more food on you?" she suddenly asks, her eyes fixated on the apple in my hand.

Takes me a moment to remember that I also brought a banana. I rummage through my bag and hand it to her. She peels it open and then looks down at my book, which has fallen onto the floor between us. She reaches and picks it up.

"Beryl Markham sure is fearless isn't she? Imagine, being the first to fly across the Atlantic. I've probably read this book at least twenty times myself," she says, turning the book over in her hands. Gently, she presses her finger on a large brown smudge on the book's spine.

"Looks like you've read this a few times, too."

The smudge was actually from our oven. I had saved all my money for a month to be able to afford the book. I had to hide it safely away from Mom and Charlotte because it was about flying. One day I was sitting in the kitchen, engrossed as Beryl is about to leave her native land of Africa for her flight across the Atlantic, when the front door opened. I was so involved in my reading, I didn't hear it. And then Mom came into the room. She had gotten off work early from her shift at the Red Cross because they ran out of bandages for her to roll.

"You're reading about flying again?" she asked, quickly grabbing it away from me. "You know how I feel about this. Why you keep insisting on defying my rules, Bernadette, is beyond me." She opened the oven door and tossed my book inside. When I snuck back into the kitchen a few hours later to retrieve it, the heat from the gaslight had cooked the spine, leaving a smoldering black mark.

Thinking about it all, I am ready to burst into tears. If the auburn-haired girl wasn't sitting in my compartment I would be able to close the door and have a nice cry. But instead, I choke back the tears.

"What's your name?" she asks abruptly.

I hate this question, because I always feel the need to offer an explanation after I answer. "Bernadette Thompson. But nobody calls me that, except my Mom. I hate it, actually. She gave me a rich sounding name, hoping it would help me get a rich husband. Everyone calls me Byrd. It's better that way."

"Byrd. I like that. So where you headed, Byrd?"

"Texas."

She laughs. "Well, that I figured. We're already in Texas, by the way. You must have slept all through Oklahoma. That's when I got on. You ain't going to Sweetwater, are you?"

I slowly nod. I didn't even know we were outside of Iowa yet.

"Me too," she says, and our eyes meet. And before I know it, the tears start streaming down my face, and for a moment I feel like I'm watching myself from outside of my body.

She sits down next to me. "What's the matter? Are you nervous about going to Sweetwater?" she asks. And then I know why I am crying.

I shake my head. "It's just that I've never met another woman pilot before," I tell her, the honesty surprising even myself. "I was convinced I was the only one, except for Amelia Earhart and Beryl Markham. That's why I'm going to Sweetwater. To find the others. To belong somewhere."

The girl nods, and when our eyes meet, I know she understands.

We sit together in silence as the train rattles on, taking us closer to our future.

CHAPTER TWO

Her name is Sadie. Sadie from Norman, Oklahoma. And she comes from brains. Both her parents are professors at the University of Oklahoma. She's even gone to college there. She seems to have everything. Smarts. Fashionable clothes. *Two* parents. If she wasn't so nice, I'd be jealous to bits.

We spend the rest of the train ride talking about airplanes and flight theory. She tells me all about her boyfriend, John, who is flying for the Allied Forces, dropping bombs over Germany. Fighting the Nazis.

"We met at an air show in Oklahoma City. I took one look at his little Cessna aircraft and was hooked—even before I caught a glimpse of him. He was hooked the minute I beat him in the competition. Never saw a woman fly before me. From that day on we were inseparable. Until he had to go overseas. He flew in the air raid over Hamburg last July. I wish they'd let us go on missions like that. But until they let us girls go into combat, I guess ferrying planes around the U.S. beats rolling bandages or collecting scrap metal and rubber."

"Excuse me, ladies."

We look up. Two men wearing Naval uniforms stand at the door of our compartment.

"We just thought you both should know that you are the prettiest girls on the entire train, and we'd be honored if we can visit with you for a little while."

Before we can respond they each take a seat beside us.

The tall one with a nice face, brown eyes, and dirty-blond hair is named Paul. The other man, Roger, is a little shorter with green eyes and deep black hair.

"So where are you girls headed?" Paul asks as he slings his arm around Sadie. She quickly moves away.

"I have a boyfriend, so keep your paws to yourself!"

"What's your story?" Roger leans over toward me.

"Yeah, where you gals headed?" Paul asks again. "Are you Army nurses?"

"Or do you work in the factories?" Roger smiles at me. "Sure is great how women are helping out with the war effort. Collecting scrap metal and darning socks and such."

Sadie raises one eyebrow at me, smiling slyly. "We're pilots," she suddenly exclaims, and I like how those words sound. *I'm a pilot*, I think to myself, enjoying the ring of those three words together.

Paul and Roger, however, erupt into spells of laughter.

"Come on now, stop pulling our legs," Paul says.

Roger slings his arm around my shoulder. I inch away, but I'm too close to the window and it's impossible to escape.

"Yeah, come on now. Women can't be pilots. Stop joking and join us in the refreshment car for a soda," he says, attempting to stroke my cheek with his finger.

Sadie snorts, "Oh, leave her alone."

Paul smiles at her. "Roger, can you imagine, some broad trying to push down on the pedal of an airplane with high heels on? It's ridiculous."

They share another laugh, but then Roger suddenly becomes quiet. He slowly reaches over and picks up my copy of *West with the Night* off the seat.

"What's this?" he asks, flipping through it.

"Just the diary of one of the best pilots around, man *or* woman," Sadie responds, getting to her feet.

"Wait," Paul says, grabbing Sadie's wrist, "Are you girls serious? You're...pilots?" he asks.

With pursed lips, Sadie breaks away from his grip. "A soda sounds good about now. You interested?" She glances down at me. I quickly nod.

"Good." Sadie winks at me. "We can talk about the proper way to darn socks."

"And collect scrap metal," I reply, smiling at her as I move Roger's arm off of my shoulder and I stand up.

"And don't bother following us, boys," Sadie remarks. "We'll just bore you to death with talk of victory gardens and how to bake a cake without having to use ration stamps for butter."

I laugh as Paul and Roger stare at us, flabbergasted. I follow Sadie out of the car.

"That was awful of me, wasn't it?" Sadie asks as we walk back toward the last car. "I just couldn't take those idiots blabbing on anymore about how girls can't fly. I had to say something."

"I wish I could do that. Just say what's on my mind," I tell her. "I never seem to think of the right words at the right time."

"Yeah, well, it's not always what it's cracked up to be. Believe you me, my mouth has a habit of getting me in trouble," Sadie says as we enter the refreshment car. We each order a soda and share a bag of popcorn.

Sadie stares out the window, watching the landscape pass us by, lost in thought. "Did you hear what First Lady Eleanor Roosevelt called us women pilots in 1942?" Sadie asks, turning toward me. I shake my head. In her best Eleanor Roosevelt impression she exclaims, " 'This is not a time when women should be patient. We are in a war and we need to fight it with all our ability and every weapon possible. Women pilots, in this particular case, are a weapon waiting to be used.' She's such a forward thinker. I hope to meet her someday. That's one of my dreams. That and flying a bomber aircraft. Imagine the horsepower! It makes me weak in the knees just thinking about it. I can't wait. What's the best flight you've ever been on? The one that changed your life and made you realize you wanted to be a pilot forever?" she suddenly asks.

Everything stops, except for my racing heart. The crash. The fire. The pain. She's already seen me cry once. I don't want her to think I'm a big baby. So I lie.

"I was practicing landings," I start. "I had already perfected two, and was on my way up for a third. And when I began to level off, the stick came off in my lap."

Sadie leans in closer and I can tell she's intrigued. There's a lump in my throat, probably guilt, but I continue anyway.

"I was only fifty feet off the ground. I tried to get the stick back in the socket, but it wouldn't work. I tried to reach across the front cockpit to the other stick, but my safety belt held me down. So I loosened the safety belt and leaned over and grabbed the other stick. Standing in the rear cockpit, I eased the nose down and leveled the ship while I climbed into the front seat. Everything was fine, except I had never flown with the front controls before. But somehow I managed to circle the field and came down with a better landing than earlier on."

Sadie leans back in her seat, a look of amazement on her face. "That really happen to you?" she asks. I nod. "Well, you're a better pilot than I am. I can't top that story," she says, smiling at me.

I want to smile back. I want to believe that the story is true. Even though I know it was just a newspaper article I read a few months ago about some girl from Florida.

I feel sick to my stomach for telling the lie, especially to a nice girl who I may become friends with. But I didn't know how to handle her question. And then I begin to think that if I can't handle one lousy question, how am I going to handle Sweetwater?

Sweetwater, Texas, is a small town about 200 miles west of Fort Worth. That's really all I know so far, except the summer is hot as heck and they have a lot of snakes and spiders. A woman there named Jackie Cochran started WASP, which stands for Women Airforce Service Pilots. She convinced General Hap Arnold, the commanding general of the entire Army Air Force, that if women took over the duties here at home, more men could be shipped overseas and into combat. After going to Great Britain and ferrying planes for the Allied forces overseas, with the support of Eleanor Roosevelt, Jackie was given the go-ahead to start her own program here in the United States. Avenger Field in

Sweetwater, Texas was hotter than the devil, and the men who had been training there couldn't handle the heat. It was the only base Jackie could secure to train the women because it was the only base nobody else wanted.

I heard about the program on a fluke. I had been sneaking around behind Mom's and Charlotte's backs for months and finally earned my private pilot's license. I would tell Mom I was going to the soda shop or the library, but instead I would head to the nearby airfield and spend hours practicing spins and turns and landings. It was the only place I felt calm, yet somehow alive at the same time—up in the sky above the Iowa cornfields. I knew that if Mom found out I was still flying, she would be worried and upset. After Pa's death, she had put that part of our lives behind her. Years ago she donated everything Pa ever owned to a homeless shelter in the next town over. Even when a plane flew over our farm, I could see her shuddering, trying to push away the memories. That's why I kept quiet.

One day, Aiken, the airfield owner's son, went flying with me and mentioned that his cousin was joining the Air Force. When I asked how long he'd be overseas, Aiken replied, "Oh no, *she's* not going overseas. She's going to Texas. Can't decide which is worse myself." And that's how I found out about the program. Aiken called his cousin who called a nearby recruiter, and we drove his tractor all the way to Des Moines the very next day for an Army interview and a health physical.

I was accepted, and I knew Mom and Charlotte would never approve of me going, let alone give me the money for the train ticket to Texas. But I knew I had to go. Something deep inside was tugging at me, telling me that no matter the risks, it was what I had to do.

I gave classes to a couple of young boys in the area who needed to log a few more hours of flying. After several months, I had the money to pay for the train ticket.

"Sweetwater. Next stop Sweeeeeeetwater, Texas." The sound of the attendant yelling brings me back into reality.

Sadie and I strain our necks to look outside the windows. The land is flatter than I thought it would be; the biggest piece of sky I have ever seen stretches out in every direction and meets the dusty red land at the horizon. No more cornfields. And not a single tree in sight.

We get off the train, and the scorching Texas sun hits us immediately. At the train's depot, Sadie buys us each a soda pop to cool off. Then we walk down Main Street toward the Bluebonnet Hotel, where we were instructed to wait for our ride to Avenger Field.

As we approach the hotel, we notice another girl sitting in front of the entranceway. With curly bright blond hair, a feminine figure covered by a fitted blue satin dress, and a dainty string of pearls cascading over her neckline, she looks like she walked off the cover of *LIFE* magazine. She sits delicately on her trunk, fanning herself with her train ticket.

"Ahoy, fellow pilot!" Sadie cheerfully calls to her as we approach. The girl takes a long, calculated moment to look us over head-to-toe, examining us before extending a hand for us to shake.

"Cornelia Wilkins. Nice to make your acquaintance," she says in a soft Southern drawl. I shake her hand, suddenly aware that my palms are scruffy and my nails unkempt.

"That all yours?" Sadie asks, motioning to the several pieces of luggage that surround Cornelia.

"Almost all of it," Cornelia replies. "Matilda is sending the rest."

"Who's Matilda?"

Cornelia turns a bright shade of pink. "My nanny."

"You have a nanny?" Sadie attempts to contain her laughter, but can't. "You're what, eighteen years old? Whatever do you need a nanny for?"

I could see the anger boiling inside of Cornelia. "Never you mind. It's rude to ask such questions when it's really none of your business."

"Well then, can I dare ask where you are from? Or is that none of my business either?" Sadie places her hands on her hips.

"Atlanta," Cornelia replies, deadpan, and then looks back toward the road.

So this is what Sweetwater would be like, all walks of life. The rich like Cornelia, the middle class like Sadie, and the poor like me from the cornfields of Iowa.

"Ah, Atlanta. Well, Miss Peach, I hate to tell you, but you're probably going to have to send more than two-thirds of your belongings back home to your nanny. If you make it past day one and don't have to go home yourself, that is," Sadie smirks. "The heat is pretty bad. And I'm sure the last thing you'd want is to burn that peaches-and-cream complexion of yours."

Cornelia glares up at Sadie. "I'm used to heat and humidity. At least Texas is dry and there is a breeze. It'll be a vacation compared to Atlanta."

"Yes, I'm sure it will be," Sadie answers. "A vacation filled with dust storms. And sagebrush. And dirt. And mosquitoes. And tarantulas. And rattlesnakes. And black widows. And copperheads…"

"I get the picture," Cornelia snaps back. "I assure you, you're not intimidating me." Her stare moves from Sadie to me. "And what do you have to say for yourself, farm girl? Are you just as rude as she is?" I open my mouth, but nothing comes out. "Oh, you're mute. Poor and mute. I hope to God there are more respectable girls at Avenger," she mutters, and looks back toward the road.

"Well, I'll be! Are those nylons you're wearing?" Sadie asks accusingly, bending down to get a better look at Cornelia's legs. "They are, aren't they?" She gasps. "Don't you know there's a nylon shortage in this country?"

Cornelia crosses her legs, trying to hide them. "I—I used a ration stamp to buy them. It's perfectly legal."

Sadie leers. "Legal, perhaps. But extremely unethical. Girls nowadays draw a line down the back of their legs with a makeup pencil so it looks like they're wearing them. Everyone donates their stockings to the war effort to make parachutes and tires. It's our duty."

Before Cornelia can respond, a weathered truck sputters toward us. It is so old and beat-up and rusty that for a moment I feel like I am back home. I look over at Cornelia, and she looks absolutely horrified.

CHAPTER THREE

Avenger Field is only a few miles from downtown Sweetwater, but the journey on that slow-moving contraption of a truck, nicknamed "The Cattle Wagon" by previous trainees, makes the ride feel like an absolute eternity.

Off in the distance, a plane is coming in for a landing on the airfield. Sadie and I lean over the side of the wagon to watch.

"I swear that's an AT-17," Sadie says, shaking her head in disbelief. "I've only seen those in books and newsreels. Imagine! We're going to fly that thing."

As we watch in awe a terrific wind blows around us, and my heart seems to dance along with it.

"Oh, AT-17s are nothing," Cornelia pipes in, matter-of-factly. "Once you learn how to handle them, they're just like any old Cub."

"You've flown one?" Sadie asks, half in awe and half jealous.

"Several times, in fact," Cornelia answers, smirking. "My brother is a top-notch pilot, and he taught me how to fly just about everything. Jackie was absolutely thrilled when I applied."

"Jackie was thrilled?" Sadie asks, as the cattle wagon comes to a halt in front of the administration building. "You know her, don't you? A friend of the family, isn't she? That's how you got in. I should have known."

Cornelia's cheeks begin to flush, and I can tell she regrets having shared this information with us. "Maybe my parents know her, but that has nothing to do with my flying abilities. I happen to have over five hundred hours of flying time logged."

Sadie puts her hands on her hips. "Well, I won the Oklahoma state cross-country competition last spring. You should have seen the beauty they let me compete in. Clocked the fastest time ever recorded by anyone, too. Man or woman."

"Well," Cornelia smugly smiles. "With those pants of yours, who could tell the difference?"

"Oh yeah, Miss Peach?" Sadie takes a threatening step forward, hands on hips. "Well, let me tell you something—"

Feeling that I should do something to change the subject and alleviate the tension, I point to a wooden plaque above the building. "Look!" I exclaim. It is a brightly-colored cartoon drawing of a young girl with wings, zipping through the air.

"That's Fifi," Sadie explains. "Short for Fifinella."

"Walt Disney drew her," Cornelia jumps in. "She's the guardian of women pilots everywhere."

A woman pokes her head out of the door to the administration building. "Come along, girls. Get your heads out of the clouds. There'll be plenty of time for that later."

We turn away from the airfield and join the other girls inside.

About fifty or so girls are crowded in the room, loudly chatting with each other. As we walk in, a few of them glance our way. Some smile and say hello. Cornelia briskly brushes past us and heads over to the other side of the room.

A petite Chinese girl with shiny, shoulder-length black hair, beautiful brown eyes, and a smooth olive complexion walks over to us.

"Hi, I'm Opal Lee. Are either of you from Boston? I'm asking everyone because my boyfriend, Daniel, is a doctor based there. I'm hoping someone might know him or anyone stationed at the hospital he's at. I have a picture I can show you."

"I wish I was from Boston or anywhere interesting," I respond, as Opal pulls out a picture of Daniel, a Chinese man sporting a military doctor's uniform.

"Oh, he's handsome," Sadie says. "I'll have to show you pictures of my John later. They're somewhere packed in my luggage. Where are you from Opal?"

"New York," Opal replies.

"No kidding?" Sadie is impressed. "A city gal!"

"Yep. Born and bred in Chinatown," Opal says.

"How exciting," I exclaim, a wave of jealousy running over me. "I've only read about New York in newspapers. I've always dreamed of going there to see the New York Follies dance. Iowa is awful boring."

"Well, just like Dorothy, you're not in Kansas, or Iowa for that matter, anymore," Opal says with a grin.

"Worse," Sadie laughs. "We're in Texas!"

"Hey! Anyone here from Texas?" Opal yells out at the other girls in the crowd.

"Yeah! Dallas!" a girl with short, curly brown hair yells back at us from across the room. Before we can make our way over to her, a single piercing whistle breaks through the chatter, quieting us all down.

We turn our attention to the front of the room, where a man clad in an Army uniform stands before us.

"Ladies, I'm Lieutenant William McCarthy. Welcome to Avenger Field. When I blow my whistle, I need you to line up in an orderly fashion by that door over there to pick up your uniforms, your bed sheets, and a pillow. Then we will assign each of you to a bay. Six girls live in a bay, so if you would like to pair up on your own choosing, that is fine. After you get settled in, we will have dinner. Lights out at ten. And let me stress the importance of getting a good night's sleep. You'll need it. Breakfast is at 6:00 a.m., then calisthenics class."

I lean over to Sadie and whisper, "What's calisthenics?"

"Physical training. Torturous chin-ups, push-ups, and such," she whispers back.

The lieutenant continues. "Then flight class, and ground school. You will learn teamwork, confidence, pride, alertness, attention to detail, discipline, and most importantly, how to fly the Army way. I know that many of you think you can already master a PT-14 or an AT-11. Well, I've got news for you. Most of you can't. And most of you won't. Your first check ride is in two weeks. At least one in three girls will wash out and be sent home immediately. Understand? Good." A shrill whistle pierces the air, and we head over toward the side of the room to wait in line for our uniforms and bedding.

My heart races when I think about what would happen if I fail. I would have to go back home to Iowa. The thought is unbearable. I look over at Sadie and Opal, who are chatting up a storm about PT-14s. A lump forms in my throat and my stomach tightens. What have I gotten myself into?

We are issued two olive-drab colored mechanics overalls in lieu of flight uniforms. They have been nicknamed "zoot suits" by the previous trainees and are simply laughable. Mine are both a size 40 and they look like potato sacks rather than flight uniforms. A 32 would have fit me better, but there weren't any smaller sizes. They are hand-me-downs from the men's division because when the women's flight training program began, Jackie Cochran didn't have the funds to afford new uniforms for the women trainees.

"I'll look like a clown wearing this!" Sadie exclaims, holding the zoot suit up to her tiny frame.

"I can fit three of me in this," Opal says as she looks down at hers, wrapping a belt around the numerous folds of fabric.

"I don't think it's fair that we get stuck with the men's old uniforms," a curly-haired girl says in a strong twangy drawl, as she strolls up to us. "Hi, I'm Deirdre."

"From Dallas, right?" Opal asks. "You were the girl who answered me when I asked if anyone was from Texas."

"Yep! But I grew up in the city. I'm used to rodeos and white picket fences and nights out on the town. Not the desert."

"Oh, let's drive to Dallas one weekend! How much fun would that be?" Opal asks, excited.

"Whoa, Nelly!" Sadie responds. "We don't even have our room assignments, and already you're talking about taking a weekend leave. You've got spunk, kid. I like that."

"I'm just…eager. I've lived in New York my whole life. Never left until now, unless you count New Jersey. I want to see everything," Opal admits.

I knew how she felt. This was my first time out of Iowa, and I was filled with thrilling uncertainty.

"Come on girls! Let's get focused. We need to get a good bay," Sadie says, breaking my concentration. "I don't want to be trapped rooming with any stuck-up drips."

"But there are only four of us, and there's six to a bay," I point out.

"There was this one girl I was talking with earlier," Deirdre says. "I'll bet she'll bunk with us. She's a little bit nervous about being here, but she's sharp as a whip. You'll like her."

Deirdre runs off to find her friend as Opal, Sadie, and I head toward the bays.

"Well, five's a good enough number. I'm sure whoever else they throw in with us will work out fine," Sadie says as she swings open the screen door to our bay.

The bays are basically one long, flat building divided by walls. A bathroom sits between every two bays, and we soon realize that twelve girls will share one toilet, one sink, and one shower.

The beds are old, the springs are rusty, and the mattresses are worn. Our sheets are scratchy and coarse, and the pillows are flat. At the foot of each bed is a small metal storage trunk. And next to the beds are metal lockers.

"How are we supposed to cram everything we own into these measly spaces?" Sadie groans as she throws her trunk down on the bed closest to the door. "I'll have to send half of my belongings back home."

"It'll be easy for me," I reply, dragging my much smaller trunk near the bed next to her. "Didn't have anything to bring. It's the first time being poor has come in handy."

"Where on earth am I supposed to hang the nice dresses I brought for nights out?" Sadie examines her locker. "There are no hangers or hooks or anything."

"Just fold them for now, and you can use hot water from the shower to steam the wrinkles out later," Opal says as she unpacks her bag next to me. "I'll show you how. I worked for a while in a Laundromat, and believe me, I know more than I care to about getting rid of stains and wrinkles."

The door swings open and Deirdre walks in. Behind her is a tall, lanky girl with dirty-blonde braids and brown eyes so big they almost pop out of her head.

"This is Jean. From Seattle. She's our fifth," Deirdre proclaims as she tosses her bag onto a bed.

"Hello," Jean says quietly, and walks over to the bed next to Deirdre's. She sits down on the edge of it, and I notice that she is holding her stomach, as if she is ill. I let go of the sheet I am putting on my mattress and walk over to her.

"Are you okay?" I ask.

Jean looks up at me, revealing tears in the corner of her eyes. But before I can say anything, suddenly she grabs her stomach, stands, and runs into the bathroom. We all stand there, motionless. And then we hear her vomiting.

She doesn't come out for several minutes, and when she does, we all turn back to making our beds and folding our clothes.

"Sorry," Jean says, as she sits down again. "My nerves are all over the place at the moment."

"I know just how you feel," Sadie says. "I'm sure as heck gonna double over before my first check ride."

Jean just nods and begins to unpack her belongings.

"Geez, it's hot!" Sadie exclaims, wiping the sweat from her brow. "Isn't it a riot to think how the men who were stationed here all requested transfers after being here only a little while? They couldn't hack the heat."

My stomach begins to growl. All I've eaten today was that apple on the train. "What do you think we'll have for dinner? I'm absolutely starving!"

"I want chicken. Or steak," Opal says, dreamily.

"Or pork chops. Gosh, it feels like I haven't had pork chops in forever. What with all the rationing and food stamps," Sadie says.

"I hope there's dessert. I miss ice cream and cake," Deirdre says.

"I'm just happy we don't have to worry about rationing anymore," I say, remembering how hard it was for us at home, especially since we had a bad crop this year and couldn't rely on our corn to bring in any income. I feel a tad guilty thinking about Mom and Charlotte, and how I'm going to be eating well when they have so little. But the thought quickly fades when the front screen door flaps open and to our surprise, a tall, handsome man wearing a flight lieutenant's uniform is standing there, carrying a large metal trunk on his shoulder. A hush falls over the bay.

"Permission to enter Bay 4?" he asks. His blue eyes sparkle down at us as we all stare up at him in awe. A moment passes before Sadie takes the initiative and steps forward.

"Yes, Sir. Of course," she says.

"Please," Opal adds, her cheeks turning bright crimson. "Come in, Sir."

The lieutenant grunts as he enters the bay, and sets the trunk down on the ground. "What do you got in that thing, Miss?" he says, as he looks behind him.

And then the worst thing in the world happens. Cornelia Wilkins floats into the room.

"Thank you, Lieutenant. You are a true hero. There was no way I could have managed to carry that across the grass all by myself."

The lieutenant crosses his arms. "For the record, Cadet, it is impolite to refer to a commanding officer by their rank. 'Sir' is sufficient. This being your first day on base, I'll let it slide. But some of your instructors won't be as forgiving."

"I'm sorry, Sir. I didn't mean any disrespect." Cornelia's cheeks turn an embarrassed shade of pink as she turns around. Seeing both Sadie and myself, she freezes, raising an eyebrow. "There must be some mistake, Sir," she says, turning back toward the lieutenant. "This can't be my bay."

"All the other bays are filled. You are the last to be assigned a room," the lieutenant declares as he swings the screen open and leaves, letting the door slam behind him.

"Well, look at what the cat dragged in," Sadie whistles, placing a hand on her hip.

Cornelia takes a long, deep breath. She walks over to Jean and Deirdre.

"Hello, I'm Cornelia." She stretches out her hand gracefully, and shakes both of their hands. And then she glances over at Opal. "Oh!" she exclaims, startled.

"Don't worry. I'm Chinese. An American. Not a Japanese spy," Opal says, laughing a bit, as if she's used to people distrusting her.

"No, I didn't think, I mean, I just—" Cornelia takes a deep breath. "It's nice to meet you." She turns around and glances at the last empty cot in the room.

"That's yours, Miss Peach," Sadie says. "I'm dying to see what sort of magic you'll use to fit all that luggage into one little locker. Specially without that nanny of yours to do it for you. I'm surprised Cochran didn't let you stay at a suite in the Bluebonnet Hotel. Isn't that more your style?"

Cornelia is fuming. She tosses her handbag onto her cot and takes a step forward toward Sadie.

"You know absolutely nothing about me, so shut your mouth! If you continue to berate me, I can guarantee I will make your life here miserable." She glances over at me. "That goes for your little farm friend, as well."

Although the news of having to live in close quarters with Cornelia horrified us, dinner sure didn't. The mess hall isn't anything fancy or impressive. Long metal tables stretch themselves out around the drab-colored room. Wooden benches surround both sides of the tables. But the food is top notch. We are each served a nice-size steak with mashed potatoes and green beans on the side. I can't believe my eyes when the kitchen staff also places a fresh roll with actual, real butter on our trays! I haven't had butter in over a year, because of the war rationing. And for dessert we have chocolate pudding. It is probably the best meal I have eaten in my entire life. No more war rationing. No more planting turnips and parsnips. We need to feed our bodies well, to keep our muscles strong.

There is hardly any talking at dinner except for some chitchat about Texas spiders and snakes. We are all so exhausted that the only thoughts in our minds are of collapsing into bed and falling asleep. And that is exactly what we do when we get back to the bay. Even Cornelia, who spends ten minutes complaining about how her bed is farthest from the window, and therefore she won't receive any air circulation, conks out when the lights go off.

CHAPTER FOUR

The air slaps every inch of my skin with pain. "Paaaaaa!" I scream, but the air finds its way into my nose, into my mouth. When I look up all I see is my parachute flapping rapidly as the wind tunnels into it, and the fire from the crash in the distance. Right before I hit the ground, I think I hear him calling me, and then the blackness comes.

I feel a hand shaking my shoulder.

"You all right, Byrdie?"

I roll over and squint. Sadie is standing above me, fully dressed. Her hair is rolled up in pink cushy hair curlers. I nod.

"You were screaming in your sleep."

I look outside the bay window. It is still dark outside.

"You better hurry if you want hot water before the girls in Bay 5 use it all up. Formation is in twenty." I moan and roll over. "Cornelia's still asleep. Want me to wake her up first instead?" Sadie asks, grinning.

Instantly I throw off the blanket and sit up, my feet hitting the hard concrete with a thud. So this is what mornings will be like at Sweetwater. I look around and take a moment to orient myself, soaking in my new morning routine.

Opal is brushing her hair. Deirdre is lacing her shoes. Jean is ironing her blouse. Sadie is taking the curlers out of her hair. And Cornelia is still sound asleep. I think about Mom and Charlotte, and I wonder what their new morning routine will be without me. It was my responsibility to wake Mom up, while Charlotte made pancakes for breakfast.

Not the kind you'd get at a restaurant. These were made with only flour and water. No syrup. No butter. No flavor. And they coated your mouth with a pasty film that managed to stay with you throughout the day.

"Hurry it up!" Sadie hollers my way, as she opens my locker and tosses my towel at me. "Shower! Now!"

Half asleep, I head to the bathroom, where a girl from the adjourning bay is coming out of the shower.

Unfortunately, there is no hot water left.

Breakfast is just as good as last night's dinner, if not better. Eggs, buttermilk biscuits, grits, and sausage are scooped onto our plates, and we devour everything in silence. I look at Cornelia out of the corner of my eye. She is sitting by herself, sulking. Her hair is still wet from the shower she had to take five minutes before formation. She looks up and scowls my way.

"Wonder if what's-his-face is going to be our flight coach," Sadie says dreamily.

"Who?" Opal asks.

"The dreamboat who helped Miss Peach with her trunk."

Cornelia suddenly slams her fork down on her plate.

"I don't know why we have to eat with our bay." She glares at Sadie, tosses a blond curl behind her shoulder, and stands up. I swear I see a small tear in her right eye begin to trickle out, but before I can be sure she turns and walks out of the mess hall.

"I hope she gets whacked with demerits," Sadie says, watching as Cornelia runs out of the mess hall, followed by an attending officer.

And at that moment, I feel truly sorry for Cornelia. I have the urge to go after her, to make sure she's all right. But before I get a chance, a whistle is blown and we all have to clear our plates.

Calisthenics class makes me want to die. We do high jumps, flutter kicks, knee benders, squats, push-ups, and chin-ups. I use muscles I never knew I had. Immediately after, around eight o'clock, we change into our ridiculous zoot suits and head out onto the airfield. Already, I'm feeling worn-out and winded. There's another bay of girls who have been assigned to train with us, and we all stand there in the sweltering Texas heat, sweaty and nervous as we wait for our flight instructor to join us.

"Oh, boy. It's hotter than the devil," Sadie says, wiping her brow with the back of her hand.

"But at least there's a breeze to dry the sweat," Opal chimes in.

A gust of wind hits my face, nice and cool until a burst of Texas sand gets stuck in my teeth. "Too bad the dust sticks to us before the wind can dry it off," I say, spitting the sand out of my mouth in several attempts.

Cornelia, who has attached herself to one of the girls from the other bay, catches me spitting, and raises her eyebrow. She whispers something to one of the other girls and they look over at me, giggling. I can just imagine how unladylike I must look, but at that moment I don't care. I can't believe I felt sorry for her at breakfast. Two men in the distance walk toward us. The first is an older man, a major, with white hair and a gruff, weathered face. And the second is the handsome young lieutenant who was in our bay the night before. As they approach, we all stand at attention, with backs straight, shoulders down, chins up.

The major takes a moment to inspect each of us. There is an intensely military bearing about him. The smile beneath his trimmed mustache is weary, his white hair is thinning, and there are lines around his eyes from squinting against the Texas sun.

"I'm Major Pickett," he tells us, "but you all call me 'Sir.' Let me just tell you something before we begin. I hate women pilots. And it would make me very happy to give a big darn 'U' to every single one of you. For those who are too dim-witted to know, a 'U' stands for an unsatisfactory mark. When you get a 'U,' you also get sent home. That means you don't got what it takes to fly these planes. It means ya stink. Now, I ain't one for thinking women should be flying in the military, and it wasn't of my choosing to be down here training you lot. But I got my orders to do just that, and unfortunately I got no choice. All I ask from you is to pay attention, work hard, and give me no lip. Is that clear?"

"Yes, Sir," we respond with nervous, shaky voices.

"You want to be pilots!" he screams at us. "That's a laugh. Sounds like y'all would rather be darning socks and painting your nails. Now, answer me again. This time, like you mean it. Is that clear?"

We all scream, "YES, SIR!"

"That's a little better. Not much, though. Now, I want you to split up into your bays. I will be training the girls in Bay 4, and Lieutenant Andrews here will be training the girls in Bay 5."

As we split up, Sadie and I give each other nervous glances. We're in Bay 4. I can see the disappointment in everyone's eyes knowing that our dreams of being with Lieutenant Handsome were not going to come true.

"Come on girls. Doesn't take all day to bake a cake. We got work to do," Major Pickett says, looking us over carefully. He points to Sadie and Opal. "You and you are together." He points at Deirdre and Jean. "You and you." And lastly, he points to Cornelia and myself. "And you and you."

"These are your assigned partners. You will be working together for the next two weeks, until your first check ride. You will be graded not only on how good of a flyer you are, but how well you work together as a team. Furthermore—"

"But, Sir," Cornelia suddenly pipes up.

Alarmed by the interruption, Major Pickett stops talking and looks straight at her. "Nobody interrupts me. Is that clear?"

"I'm sorry, Sir, but I was under the understanding that we don't fly with a buddy for several weeks. I'm just wondering, what is the point of having a partner if we're going to be soloing?"

Major Pickett smiles, scratches his chin, and then looks up at the hot Texas sun and squints. "Why do you ask?"

Cornelia takes a moment to calculate her thoughts. "I have a problem failing because of someone else's shortcomings." She glances in my direction. "She's the type that'll wash out. I just know it. Look at her. She's petrified."

I can feel my cheeks start to flush and my hands grow numb. How dare she say something like that in front of everyone! Sadie was right. Cornelia is a stuck-up drip.

"I'm afraid that's the Army way," Major Pickett roars at her, inches away from her face. "And if you don't like it, then GO HOME!" He steps back and paces back and forth, looking us each in the eyes. "You need each other, and it's my job to teach you that you do. If you think you're here to be the best, to be better than everyone else, you made a mistake. Shoulda stayed back home and flown state competitions if you want applause and flowers thrown at you. Listen to me when I say this. You're here because the men are over there, defending this country from the German and Japanese forces. Plain and simple. And let me tell y'all something else. The men over there would die for each other. I've never met a woman pilot who'd die for another, 'cept maybe Jackie Cochran herself, and none of y'all are fit to wipe her boots." He spits on the hot concrete, right in front of Cornelia. "You're free to leave anytime, cadet. You're also free to prove me wrong. It's your choice." He pauses a moment before breaking into a small smile. "Now let's see what you lot got. From the looks of it, I ain't expectin' much."

CHAPTER FIVE

ajor Pickett takes everyone up one at a time. When it's my turn, my heart starts racing. I climb into the cockpit when the major tells me to. I quickly say a prayer and try my hardest to remember everything on the checklist. I move the controls freely, check the flaps, check the trim, but when I begin to run up the engine, the major's voice bellows in my ear.

"No! No! No! No! NO!" He screams. I immediately freeze. "You didn't set the props for take off!" I gulp, trying harder to focus and not look over at Cornelia, who I'm sure is smiling at my mistake. "You want to go home in a body bag your first week of flying?" I quickly shake my head. "Then next time, don't be so careless." He opens the cockpit door, and exits the aircraft. That is it. We don't fly.

I feel like crying. Like ripping the heavy zoot suit off and throwing it in the can. Maybe I'm not as good as I thought. Maybe they made a mistake choosing me. Maybe I don't have what it takes to fly the Army way. I look around at the other girls standing there watching as I unbuckle my safety belt and climb out. Sadie walks forward and gives me a hug. I try hard not to cry, but I am unable to hold the tears in. I am tired and hungry and miss Pa more than anything in the world and wish it were him hugging me instead.

We eat lunch and then go to ground school, which consists of two different classes we have to take every day. Our first class, flight theory, seems easy. I have always had a good head for math and understand the basic principles of gravity and how things fly. Pa taught me about how an aircraft's thrust and lift must be sufficient to overcome its weight when I was younger. The second class, engines, seems harder, and I hope to be able to squeak by with a B.

We have about two hours after class before dinner, so Sadie, Opal, and I decide to go explore downtown Sweetwater before finishing our homework. We change into our civilian attire, which is a fancy way of saying all non–military-issued clothing. I feel a little self-conscious about wearing my tattered old clothes, so Sadie lends me a yellow blouse and a red scarf to tie around my neck. Opal shows me how to curve my hair into an elegant French twist, and then she applies a smear of dark red lipstick to my lips. When I look at myself in the bathroom mirror, I feel older.

It is hot as Hades, but the cool breeze feels good as we walk toward the long stretch of road that we're hoping will take us to town.

"Major Pickett really is horrid, isn't he?" Opal says.

"Yep," Sadie agrees. "Just our luck to get stuck with Ol' Pick instead of the cute one. Probably God's way of reminding me I'm already spoken for."

"What's John like?" I ask her, imagining he's probably handsome, smart, and a stellar pilot, just like Sadie.

She looks up at the sky as an AT-6 flies overhead. "That. That is how he makes me feel. You know that fluttering feeling you get when you hear an engine rumbling? When the horsepower goes from 65 to 650 in a split second? That is exactly how John makes me feel. Next to flying, he's the love of my life, and I miss him like the dickens. I keep imagining what it'll be like when I see him again. I save every letter he sends. I treasure every picture. Someday I'll be able to show them to our kids, and they'll know what he's doing for his country."

"Not to mention what you're doing—" Opal starts to say, but instead her words are replaced by a high-pitched scream. She quickly runs to the other side of the road. I turn to look and in the brush, off to the side of the road, a rattlesnake is watching our every move. Slowly, Sadie and I step away. We can hear the rattling of its tail as it stares in our direction. Its tongue slithers in and out of its mouth as it glides toward us.

When I was little, my sister found a rattlesnake in our washroom. It had crawled through the pipes and came out through the water faucet. She came running out, screaming and crying, mistakenly leaving the door open behind her and allowing the snake to run free through our kitchen. I was only six or seven then. We were home alone. Pa was at the airfield, and Mom was taking care of a sick elderly woman in town. Our closest neighbors were miles away.

Charlotte refused to go back inside, so we sat on our front porch for hours, waiting for someone to come home. When Pa's Chevy came clanking toward us in the distance, we ran out to meet him, screaming about the snake, and that Mom was gone, and how we were going to sleep outside if he didn't kill it.

He scooped us up in his arms, telling us everything would be all right. Then he went out back and got his shovel. We watched, holding our breaths, as he walked into the house. Then he told us to follow him.

Cautiously, Charlotte and I held hands as we tiptoed into the house. In the kitchen, Pa picked up the old metal canister Mom used to dispose of chicken guts and unwanted cow entrails when she cooked. He began to tap the floorboards with the shovel. He opened the cupboards, checked under the table, and as he was going to look behind the oven, Charlotte clenched my hand harder than she ever had.

She opened her mouth, but nothing more than a squeak came out. Her eyes, filled with fear, were practically popping out of her head. She managed to raise an arm and pointed meekly toward the window curtains.

The snake was sitting on the windowsill. Pa grabbed the canister and placed it underneath. When the snake began to slither to the side, he used the shovel to prevent it from escaping toward the counter. Instead, he picked it up with the shovel and quickly but gently placed it into the canister, and then carefully topped it with the lid. He made it look easy.

Charlotte and I had been holding our breaths the whole time, our hearts racing a million beats per second. Pa turned to us, holding the canister in his hands.

"You didn't kill it!" Charlotte exclaimed, finally able to speak again.

"Killing a snake is far more dangerous than capturing it. A snake lashes out and bites when it's faced with the threat of death. Why should he be denied a chance for survival just because he is unwanted? It is better this way, my darlings. Remember that."

I know what to do. Off to the side of the road is a wooden stick. I cautiously back up, bend down, and pick it up.

"Sadie, give me your purse," I demand. She hands it to me. I open it and take out her wallet and tube of lipstick. I give them back to her.

Off in the distance, a cloud of dust is heading toward us. "Someone's coming!" Opal exclaims. She waves her hands in the air for help.

"Don't move," I whisper. "You'll upset it."

I take a step toward the snake. I reach out with the stick. It examines it, uncertain. Then it begins to rub up against it. I slowly pull upward, and the snake coils itself around the wood.

I hear the grumbling of the vehicle and look over. A truck is approaching, but I ignore it and focus on my next move. I hold Sadie's bag open and slowly hold it out. With one swift, yet gentle move, I place the snake inside and quickly set it on the ground. With the stick, I press the purse latch closed, and then stand there, allowing my heartbeat to slow down.

I turn and look at Sadie and Opal, who are staring at me, speechless.

"Wait till everyone hears about this," Sadie exclaims, running toward me. "That has got to be the finest thing I've ever seen someone do. I cannot wait to see Cornelia's face when she hears about this."

"Well done." A man's voice breaks my concentration. I had forgotten all about our visitor in the truck. We turn, and there he is. Lieutenant Andrews. Lieutenant Handsome. And he is walking toward me.

"How did you know how to do that?" He looks at me with luminous eyes, small planets floating in vast blue skies.

"Iowa has snakes too, Sir," I reply.

"That's true." He looks down at me. "What's your name, cadet?" he asks.

I pause a moment, before realizing I have to answer him. "B-Bernadette…um…I mean Byrd. Byrd Thompson," I say, my voice squeaking a tad.

"Oh." An odd expression washes across his face. "I see."

I quickly look away, and down at the purse on the ground. "Sorry about your purse, Sadie."

"Living is worth the sacrifice," she says flippantly.

Lieutenant Andrews picks the purse with the snake in it up off the ground. "I know of an area about twenty miles away where I can set him free. A little stretch of desert uninhabited by people." He looks over at me again. "Very impressive, cadet. You should use some of that fearless determination during flight training."

I smile and nod, quickly looking away. I feel like an absolute mess. My hands are sticky. My blouse is untucked. Sweat is pouring from the sides of my face.

"Where you soldiers headed?" he asks.

"Into town," Sadie replies. "We want to explore Sweetwater."

"I see," he says. "Well, it's a good thing I ran into you. You would have been walking for ages. Get in and I'll give you a lift."

CHAPTER SIX

Lieutenant Andrews drops us off at the post office and tells us he will pick us up in an hour and drive us back to Avenger, giving him just enough time to release the snake and for Sadie, Opal, and I to explore the town.

We soon realize that there isn't much to do in downtown Sweetwater. There's a movie theater, a swimming pool, a soda shop, a Sears and Roebuck department store, and not much else. We step into the soda shop and order root beer floats at the counter. A heavyset man and his two scrawny children sit at a nearby booth and stare at us. An elderly woman eyes us disapprovingly. A group of young boys glance at us suspiciously.

"Everyone's staring at us," Sadie whispers. "It feels peculiar. Like we're doing something wrong. It's not like there's alcohol in here or anything," she says, taking a sip of her float.

"I know what they're staring at," Opal says, nervously looking around. "It happens all the time. They don't know what I am. It's a mystery to them. And I'm sure they're not used to seeing Asians of any kind down here in Texas."

"For goodness sake, stop staring at her! She's Chinese-American!" Sadie loudly declares at everyone and then turns back to us. "Oh, who cares about them? Lieutenant Handsome is so… handsome," she says.

"What about John?" I ask her.

"John? Who's John?" Sadie giggles and twirls around on her stool. "I'm kidding. I'm crazy about John. Poor John." She sighs, nervously. "I wonder what he's doing right now."

"Whatever it is, let's hope it's better than what Deirdre's brother has to endure," Opal says, and shakes her head.

"Why? What's the story?" Sadie inquires.

"P.O.W. Prisoner of War. His name's Leonard. I think he's in Italy, but I'm not sure. She's trying to keep a good face about it. Doesn't let herself think the worst, but I know she's awful worried. Said that the reason she's here is so she can free up a male pilot for combat overseas, and who knows, that pilot may be the one who rescues her brother."

"I can't imagine," Sadie says. "She hasn't received any word?"

Opal shakes her head. "Nothing. They hardly ever mention anything about POWs in the paper, either."

"Can you believe our training manual actually discouraged us from reading the papers? They don't want us knowing what's going on overseas. Afraid we'll get cold feet." Sadie stands up, reaching for a copy of *The Sweetwater Reporter* from across the counter and gives the cashier a dime. "I, for one, won't be able to stop reading the headlines until John is back on American soil."

"What's it say?" Opal asks as we lean over, scanning the front page. The papers scare me. Every time I read about someone dying I can only think about his family and how life will never be the same for them.

"The German army is deep in Russia and fighting is still intense in northern Africa and the Asian Pacific," Sadie reads aloud. "Listen to this. The United States is spending more than a hundred million dollars a day on the war effort. A hundred million dollars!"

"I bet it cost millions of dollars to build each of the planes we're flying," Opal says.

"Not quite that much," Sadie replies. "But close. I read that the Boeing B-29 Superfortress, our country's biggest bomber to date, costs about $650,000 to build. It has a wing span of a hundred and forty-one feet and can fly a maximum speed of three hundred and fifty-seven miles per hour! Imagine having the opportunity to fly something that fast and expensive."

"Even with the millions they're spending every day, they still don't have enough money to cover all of the costs," Opal says, looking up from the paper. "In his last letter, Daniel mentioned that there is a severe shortage of medicine overseas. Some hospitals don't even have enough blankets for all the patients. Often, in cold climates, they die of frostbite. I'm scared to death Daniel is going to have to go over there soon."

"What about you, Byrdie?" Sadie asks. "Do you have a fella fighting overseas?"

I shake my head no.

"Well, then, it's settled."

"What is?" I ask, apprehensively.

"You and Lieutenant Handsome," Sadie says. "Was I imagining it, or did you two have a moment after you caught that snake?"

Opal nods. "They had a moment."

"No, we did not!" I gasp. "And dating an instructor's forbidden! You know very well Jackie Cochran has strict rules against that. Avenger isn't nicknamed Cochran's Convent for no reason. Besides, there's no time for dating."

"Goodness, Byrdie, you're blushing!" Opal notices.

"You're rosier than an apple," Sadie says, laughing.

"It's just a sunburn. I'm not used to the Texas sun yet," I answer, although I admit that my face feels warmer than normal. "Now if you'll excuse me, I have to use the ladies' room."

I splash water on my face and take a few breaths to calm my racing heart. I am here to fly, nothing more, I tell myself. The only thing that matters is flying, especially now that I performed horribly at flight training this morning. I silently promise myself to eat, sleep, and breathe flying from here on out.

The next morning, I am the first one up. The first one to shower, to dress, to make my bed, to sweep around my floor area. When I am done I sit on my bed and go over the flight checklist, memorizing all of the cockpit procedures for the PT-19A, the primary trainer that we are flying today.

Even when everyone else begins to wake up, I concentrate solely on the flight procedures.

At breakfast, I sit at the end of the table, going over everything for what feels like the hundredth time. Sadie sits across from me, quizzing me.

"I wish we could be partners," I tell her. "Cornelia makes me nervous."

"Don't let her pull anything," Sadie says. "If you feel that she's mocking you, ignore her. You do not want to jeopardize your performance. Focus on the cockpit procedures. Listen to Major Pick's instructions carefully. And forget about Cornelia. All she has to do is keep a record of how many spins and stalls you do, and what your highest altitude is. Now, let's get back to work. How many inches do you crack the throttle before takeoff?"

We sit in the ready room, waiting to fly. My stomach is an absolute mess. Off in the distance, Opal is coming in for her landing. She is flawless, which makes me even more nervous because it is my turn next.

I check to make sure I have everything—goggles, my parachute pack, the lucky rabbit's foot that Sadie let me borrow.

"Remember," Sadie says, poking my arm. "Just have fun. This is what you came here for. To fly a plane like that." I smile. She's absolutely right. Pa once told me that the best pilot is the one who loves to fly more than anything else in the world. It doesn't matter if you can master the controls or fly straight; if your heart is not in it, you might as well be driving a car.

Opal hops out of the plane, and Cornelia and I head out to the field.

"Don't forget to check for snakes," Cornelia says with a smirk on her face.

My face reddens with anger but I ignore her and climb the side of the plane, swinging myself into the cockpit.

"Miss Thompson, I hope for your sake you are able to actually start this thing this time. If not, I may need to hand out an early check ride failure," Major Pickett says.

"Sir, I wouldn't give you the pleasure of sending me home," I respond, and I swear he actually cracks a smile.

I check Form 1. As I pick up the safety belt, I call out the gas supply in each tank for Cornelia to record. I fasten the belt, adjust the seat till I'm comfortable. I plug in the earphones and check that the radio switch is off. I adjust the rudders and unlock the controls. I'm about to flap up, then remember I have to set the parking brakes.

When the brakes are set, I flap up and adjust the rudder to three degrees. I trim the tab to zero and make sure the gas is on reserve. I crack the throttle three-fourths of the way. Then I check the instruments. I am ready.

I gently wobble the pumps to four pounds, and then energize to peak.

"All clear!" I yell out for Cornelia to record. She backs away. I wait until the oil pressure is up to fifty pounds, and then I prop forward. I turn the radio on, and then the engine.

The altimeters are set. The throttle is fully open, and I am ready for takeoff. We are roaring down the flight line, and this is it. The climb. I ascend slowly and steadily, mounting upward until the mags read 2,100 R.P.M. I switch to the fuller tank of gas, and then crank the flaps up.

And just like that I am cruising. I look over the side down at the world below as the air gently hits my face. That glorious feeling of flying takes over my body, and my nerves instantly calm down. The engine roars and I can feel the vibrations through my body, almost instructing me on how to handle the aircraft. It feels smoother than anything I've ever flown before.

"Take her a mile west and then south. We're going to do some turns," the major yells at me.

I steer west and then south. I look out around me. The clouds above me are perfect and fluffy. The Texas sun is glistening in the distance. The breeze against my face feels absolutely divine. The earth below is big and colorful. I always love looking down, and thinking about how there are so many places to explore and people to meet. I feel at peace. That is until Ol' Pick decides to do just that—pick on me a bit.

"You didn't reduce the power quick enough," he bellows. "And you went out too far before making the turn."

I refocus and do another turn, this time tightening it up a bit.

"Better. Now, let's see some figure eights," he demands. I comply, turning and twisting like a dance you never want to end.

But then he asks me to dive. My heart starts pounding, and the calmness dissipates. I dive, and it's a bit shaky. And Major Pick's screaming in my ear isn't helping much. I always freeze up before dives. I hate how empty they make my stomach feel. Eventually, I am able to pull us out of the dive and back into cruising.

"Okay, that was horrendous," he says. "Let's see if you know how to land," he says.

I love landing a plane. It's different every time. You control everything. The angle you come down from. How smooth or rough the wheels hit the ground. You can either manhandle the plane and bring it down swift and hard, or you can take your time, which I like to do, and gently touch down slow and smooth.

I switch the gas to reserve, and move the propeller to low pitch. I place the flaps at twenty degrees, and we begin to descend.

I set the parking brakes, which Pick makes a point to tell me I did too early. I ignore the criticism as I check the throttle. I switch the propeller back to high pitch. And with an even transition, the wheels meet the flight line and we land. Not bad.

I switch off the engine and lock all controls. Sadie, Opal, and the others are waving at me from the ready room, and I can't help but smile when I open the cockpit and climb out.

"Highest altitude?" Cornelia asks as I pass her.

"Seventeen thousand above sea level," I tell her. She writes it down. I stop and turn around. "Don't forget to subtract Sweetwater's sea level. I believe it is 2,376," I remind her with a smirk, and then walk away.

In the ready room, Sadie and the others pat me on the back.

"He was watching you," Opal whispers.

"Who?"

Opal motions toward the hanger, and I turn to look. Lieutenant Andrews is pointing at a map and talking to the girls in Bay 5.

I toss my goggles at Opal. "Stop pulling my leg."

"Better get back out there. It's Miss Peach's turn," Sadie says, rolling her eyes.

Cornelia, amazingly, is a very good flyer, but as expected, she shows off too much. She throws a few extra spins and stalls into her rotation. And her dives are flawless. But her landing is a little shaky, which I secretly enjoyed. I stand there and take notes, and when she's done I ask for her altitude.

Back in the ready room, Jean and Deirdre prepare to go up next. Sadie hands me a soda, and I collapse on the bench next to her. Cornelia sits at the other side, pulls a makeup compact out of her pocket, and begins to powder her nose.

"What happened on your landing, Miss Peach?" Sadie asks. "You drop your compact?"

"It wasn't my fault. The seat came loose and I shifted back a few inches. It took me by surprise, that's all," she says as she applies a smear of lipstick.

"Oh, that's nothing!" Sadie chimes in. "Hey Byrd, tell them about the time the stick came off in your lap fifty feet from landing."

I freeze. She was talking about the story I told her on the train when we first met. The story I lied about.

"They don't want to hear it," I say, taking another gulp of soda.

"Sure they do. You should be proud. It's a great story." It was too late. Sadie was surely going to tell everyone.

"The stick came off in her hand and she had never used the front controls before. She had to shimmy her safety belt off, stand up, and lean forward to work the front stick because the back one was busted. Turns out, the landing was better than all the others before, wasn't it?"

I nod, and look down at the floor.

"How remarkable!" Cornelia chimes in. I look over at her, suspiciously. "Did that really happen to you?" she asks me.

I nod.

"I underestimated you Bernadette," she says and I cringe at the sound of my full name coming from her lips. "Perhaps you do have what it takes after all," she says, smiling at me as she closes her makeup compact with a click.

We are lounging around the bay, relaxing from the hard day's work, when there is a knock at the door. Opal jumps off her bed to answer it.

An upper-class pilot stands at our door, holding a bunch of envelopes tied together with string.

"Bay 4. Here you go."

"Mail!" Opal squeals. "Oh, I wonder if Daniel wrote me." She grabs the letters and flips through them. "Here it is! From Major Daniel Wong. Boston, Massachusetts." She takes the letter out and clutches it to her heart. "It even smells like him." She sits down in the corner of the room, reading it to herself.

Sadie opens up a letter from her mother. Deirdre and Jean also open their mail. Neither Cornelia nor I receive anything. I go back to reading one of Sadie's fashion magazines, trying to ignore the other girls.

I don't expect Mom or Charlotte to write me, but it hurts more than I thought it would. Sadie notices that I am letterless and jumps onto the bed next to me.

"My mother is such a loon. She bought me all these skirts and blouses. She just can't get used to the idea that we wear fat men's overalls all day long. I'm going to have to write back and beg her not to send them. Where on earth would I put them?" Sadie says with a laugh. "What's your family like?"

I take a moment to think about it. "My mom is a hard worker, and she probably hasn't had a day off in years. My sister hates that we are poor. She can't meet a decent man and is scared to death that she'll die an old spinster."

"Oh, everyone is scared of that," Cornelia joins in as she rummages around her bed for something. "That's why we doll ourselves up every morning. Has anyone seen a black and white saddle shoe? I can only find one." She holds up the one she does have. We all shake our heads no.

She rummages through the contents of her locker and pulls it out. "Here it is." She slips it on.

"Where are you going?" Sadie asks.

"Library. I just want to look something up," she says, smiling my way. "See you girls at dinner," she says as she leaves.

"That was strange. She's all nice and chipper," I say.

"Must have banged her head on that shaky landing," Sadie replies.

"No. This can't be happening," says Opal, who is sitting on the floor in the corner with her letter from Daniel, her hand over her mouth.

"What is it?" I ask, standing up.

Tears slide their way down Opal's cheek as she reads the letter out loud.

> *My Dearest Opal,*
>
> *I want so much to know how you are getting along and whether you have had the chance to fly yet. On my end, I've been working around the clock, treating the patients who are being sent home with broken bones, gunshot wounds, and in many extreme cases, paralysis. Tonight, halfway through my shift I was called into my captain's office for a chat. You're not going to like what I have to tell you. Darling, I've received orders to report to a hospital in London in less than a week. There's a severe shortage of military doctors to care for the number of injured men who are admitted every day for treatment. I hope this news won't upset you too much. I want nothing else than to know you are happy. Every time I see an airplane fly overhead, I will think of you, and it is my wish that your heart is dancing somewhere out there, high above the earth, thinking of me.*

Opal looks up at us, her face stained with tears. "I knew this moment would come. I'm lucky he's been stationed in the states for so long. But still, it doesn't make it any easier."

"How did you two meet?" I ask, sliding down next to her on the floor.

Opal wipes a tear away. "Oh, that's a long story."

"Come on, tell us!" Sadie insists. "You never talk about New York."

"Or how you began flying, for that matter," Deirdre chimes in as she sits up in bed.

Opal sighs. "You really want to know?"

We nod.

Opal takes a deep breath and begins. "When I was little, my father was a merchant. He traveled all around the world on business. One summer he went to Mexico and came down with cholera. He died within a day. He left us with a good amount of money, so Mother and I opened a Laundromat in the storefront below our Chinatown apartment. That's where I met Daniel. He was the resident doctor at a nearby hospital. He would come into our shop and drop off his clothes every Friday afternoon. He would tell me all about medical school, and hospital life, and all the places he'd traveled to throughout the years. He didn't seem to mind that I was just some girl who worked in a Laundromat.

"A few weeks after the attack on Pearl Harbor, Mother came into my room screaming and frantically shaking me out of bed. It was around three o'clock in the morning. She told me to get dressed at once. When I looked out the window, I knew why. Our building was on fire. We had to climb down the fire escape with dozens of other families who also lived there. By the time the fire department got there, the fire had taken over the entire block. The Chinese restaurant next door was in ruins. There was nothing left of our Laundromat. Hundreds of people were standing across the street with us, watching as our lives burned to a crisp before our eyes. It was the only time I saw Mother cry.

"We found out later that it was a group of angry white street kids who set fire to the building. They blamed us for the attack on Pearl Harbor, even though we had nothing to do with it. Even though we were American.

"The next day was a Friday, and Daniel came by to drop off his laundry like he always did. When he saw what had happened, he insisted that we stay at his apartment as long as we needed. He wouldn't take no for an answer. We stayed there for several months until we could get back on our feet. Daniel made good money, and on the weekends he would take us for dinner or to the movies. We fell in love. Eventually, Mother got us both jobs as waitresses at a nearby Chinese restaurant and when we could afford to, we moved into a small studio apartment.

"But Daniel and I still saw each other after we moved out. One of his many hobbies was flying. One weekend, we met up with a friend of his who flew for the Chinese Air Force, and he took us flying in his small Cub. It was the first time I had ever been in an airplane, and I instantly wanted to learn how to fly myself. I guess I saw it as a way out of the Chinatown ghetto, which was what I wanted more than anything at the time. Seeing that I was enthusiastic and serious about learning to fly, Daniel insisted on paying for me to attend an aviation school in New Jersey. I was the only woman among fifty or so men who were registered in classes. And I fell in love with it.

"Soon after I received my private pilot's license, Daniel had to enlist in the Army, and he was shipped to Boston a few months later to treat injured soldiers who had been hurt in combat overseas. Before he left, he told me he loved me, and asked me to wait for him to come home. I agreed, knowing that he was the person I wanted to spend the rest of my life with. He made me feel important and safe.

"I heard about the WASP program at Sweetwater through a nearby recruiting officer who had gotten my information from the Jersey school. I couldn't believe that I had the opportunity to learn to fly bigger and better planes, and the government was going to pay me for it! I never imagined that I'd be able to make a living doing something I loved. Mother was against me going initially, but she knew that there was nothing for me in the old neighborhood, which was increasingly growing even more dangerous with hate crimes. Eventually she gave me her blessing, and I enrolled as soon as I could."

Opal sighs, and we sit there in silence for a moment. "And the rest you already know," she says, looking up at us.

"And your mother? Is she still in New York?" I ask.

"Yes. She's still working at the restaurant. Her English isn't that good, and I can speak Chinese but writing it is a different story, so it's hard to keep in touch. And now Daniel's leaving…"

Her words trail off as she sits, her arms folded around her legs. Sadie and Deirdre stare off, lost in a cloud of misery and sorrow. I know all of their hearts are aching for the same reason, and for a moment I am secretly happy that I don't have a boyfriend or brother overseas to worry about.

Cornelia is suspiciously not at dinner, which consists of roast beef sandwiches, green beans, and one of my favorites, corn-on-the-cob.

"She'll get demerits, for sure," Sadie says. "She already has five for running out of the mess hall yesterday. I wonder what she's up to." She takes a bite of her sandwich.

"Nothing good, I'm sure," I say, looking at the others. I notice Opal's plate is untouched. "Opal, aren't you going to eat anything?"

"I can't," Opal says, her voice shaky. "My stomach is queasy. I can't stop thinking about Daniel. I'm scared to death. I feel like I should be doing something."

"But you are doing something," Deirdre insists, taking a sip of milk. "You're taking over a job here, so that a male pilot can go overseas. The more girls that fly, the quicker the war will be over, and the sooner the men will come back home."

Opal nods, but I can tell she's still shaken up. "I think I'm going to knit a blanket to send him. With the winter coming soon, I want to know he's warm enough to endure the London cold. I would love it if you all want to chip in and help me with some of the squares."

"I'd be glad to," Cornelia says as she squeezes herself next to Sadie. "You'll have to teach me how. I've never had to make my own clothes before, so my knitting abilities are rather slim."

We all watch her like a hawk as she eats her roast beef.

"What are you up to, Miss Peach?" Sadie asks suspiciously. "And why are you so chipper?"

Cornelia takes her time chewing, swallowing, taking a sip of water, and wiping off her mouth daintily with a napkin. "Funny you should ask," she says. She reaches into her pocket and produces a piece of paper. Then she turns to me. "Either you also go by the name Diana Peters, from Avon Park, Florida, or I've caught you in a fib!"

She unfolds the paper. It is a Florida newspaper article. The headline reads, "Stick Comes Loose, But Girl Flyer Climbs Over Seat and Lands Plane."

I am silent as everyone else reads on. When Sadie looks up at me, her eyes searching my face for an explanation, I know that I am about to lose it. I quickly stand up, grab my tray, and walk away from our table.

CHAPTER SEVEN

I spend the rest of the evening pacing around the airfield, waiting until the very last minute to go back to the bay for lights out.

In the distance, a few AT-17s are coming in from night flying. I watch as they land gracefully. The AT-17 is a beautiful machine, and I want more than anything to be flying one right now. To be able to soar away and leave all my problems behind.

"Sure are beauties, aren't they?" a voice creeps up behind me. I turn around. It's Lieutenant Andrews. But for some reason, I don't feel the same flutter in my heart as before.

I nod, looking out at the airfield. "I wish I were there right now, sitting in the plane, coming in from a landing."

He smiles. "You know who that is in there?"

I shake my head.

"Just about the best darn pilot this country has, man or woman. Jackie Cochran, herself."

I watch as the cockpit door opens. A male pilot descends and then turns back around, extending his hand. Then she steps out, all glamorous, like a movie star. Her uniform is top-notch, a navy blue skirt and blazer with a matching hat atop her strawberry-blond curls, which frame her face just perfectly. She carries a blue overcoat on her arm. And her smile has enough sparkle to light up the entire airfield.

"Want to meet her?" Lieutenant Andrews whispers in my ear.

"No...I..."

"Come on," he tugs at my arm. I follow him over to where several of Avenger Field's flight instructors surround Miss Cochran, asking her how her flight was. Lieutenant Andrews pushes me close to her and extends his arm out.

"Miss Cochran, it is a pleasure to see you again, Ma'am," he says sweetly. "I just wanted to introduce you to a young lady from the newest group of trainees, Byrd Thompson. Byrd had a great flight today, and I'm sure she'll be one of our finest. She's also one heck of a snake charmer." He winks at me.

Miss Cochran looks me over and I wish to God that I had put on lipstick or some sort of makeup to make myself look more sophisticated.

"Here," she says, and tosses her long navy blue overcoat on me. "You can manage that, can't you? I am dead tired and going to bed, everyone. I'll answer all of your questions tomorrow."

Then she walks off toward the general's quarters. I am flabbergasted, but then remember that I have her coat. I run after her, following a few steps behind.

We reach the barracks, and she turns to me. "I can take it from here, thank you," she says. I hand it back to her. "How are things going?" she asks, her face softening a little.

"Fine," I answer.

"Who's your instructor?"

"Major Pickett."

"Ah, Ol' Pick. He hates women pilots. He is good, though. Pushes you. Where did you grow up?"

"Iowa," I answer.

"Pretty state. What part?"

"Outside of Des Moines."

"I've flown those parts. What did you say your name was?"

"Byrd Thompson. Actually, Byrd is short for Bernadette."

"Are you Fletcher's kid?"

My heart stops. Dad. I nod.

"I knew him well. Great pilot. It was a shame to hear about the crash. Wait, were you the daughter who was with him in the plane? I remember reading about that in the paper."

I nod again.

She looks down at me with eyes that are brown and wise, and then glances over at the airfield. "Did you know that over twenty-five thousand women applied to my program, all of them willing to fly for their country at a moment's notice?" she asks. "We could only accept a handful. To make it this far is remarkable. I know that your father would be proud of you."

"I'm lousy at dives," I suddenly admit. "They're the only thing that makes me nervous. I just can't seem to master them. No matter how hard I try."

She places her hand on my shoulder. "If you believe in yourself, you can do anything you put your mind to. Take me for instance. I was born and raised a poor orphan in Florida. I don't even know the exact day or year of my birthday. Imagine that. Now I am the fastest pilot in the world. Anything you want to do, you can do. Anything. If you believe it, you can do it. Don't let anyone tell you that you can't, that you aren't good enough. Because the sky's the limit, kid. And sometimes you've just got to sit back and ask yourself how high you want to take yourself."

"Pa, I mean, Fletcher always said he was going to make me the next Amelia Earhart. I guess that's why I'm here," I tell her. "That's what drives me."

"You can't just be doing this for someone else. You've got to want it, too." She looks up at the sky, which is pitch-black and speckled with stars. "I'll never forget the time when both Amelia and I entered a prestigious race called the Bendix. You know what happened? We were told we couldn't participate because we were women. It was 1935, and aviation was reaching new heights every day. The Wright brothers paved the way and the airplane industry was booming. And there was a handful of us women who wanted a piece of the action. Now, I for one believe that an airplane can't tell the difference between a man and a woman—only a good pilot from a bad one. And Amelia felt the same way. So we signed a protest. Eventually an agreement was reached, and we were allowed to race. Amelia placed fifth. Better than me. I didn't finish that year. There were technical problems with my plane. It wasn't until 1938, the year after Amelia's plane vanished, that I placed first.

And I had the fastest time ever logged in the record books then, man or woman. I always knew Amelia had something to do with it, that she was watching over me in some way. But it was ultimately up to me to perform. It was my heart that won. Because I wanted it."

I nod and look down at the ground. Was this something I wanted, or was it all for Pa? I don't know the answer.

"Well, best get to bed young lady," Jackie says. "Isn't it past lights out?"

The night guard gives me my first demerit for being out too late, which means I'll have to spend all of Saturday scrubbing the bathrooms. When I creep back into the bay, everyone is in bed and the lights are off. I undress, slip into my nightgown, and slide into bed. The minute my head hits the pillow I hear someone whisper my name.

I look up. Sadie is lying awake in bed. "I just want you to know," she whispers, "we put syrup in Cornelia's shampoo. She'll be a sticky mess come morning. She had no reason for doing what she did."

I lay back down, pulling the covers over my head. "I don't want to talk about it," I mumble.

"Why'd you lie to me?" Sadie sits up and folds her arms.

I sigh and turn over, watching a few flies dart from place to place on the ceiling. "I didn't know what to say. You seemed to have it all. Maybe I was a tad jealous. Maybe I wanted you to like me. Or maybe I just wanted to forget about what happened."

"What do you mean?" Sadie asks.

I pause a moment, closing my eyes. "When I was ten my Pa took me flying. I begged for him to take me up with him that morning. I begged for him to do a dive. But the engine blew."

I wrapped my arms around Pa's neck as he leaned down, kissed my cheek, and told me to be brave. That everything would be okay. And for a split-second, I truly believed him. But when I looked up at his face, there was fear in his eyes, and for a moment I didn't even recognize him. I held onto him tightly as we jumped.

"I feel just awful," Sadie murmurs when I finish telling her everything. "I can be so outspoken at times. It's a problem, I know. I blurt out what's on my mind, and often end up with a foot in my mouth. I'm so sorry, Byrdie."

"Can I ask you something?"

She nods.

"Why are you here?"

She takes a moment to think about this. "I guess I initially joined for John. I needed to do something, anything, to help with the war effort, in hopes that he'd be back home sooner. Now that I'm actually here, I guess the thrill of being one of the first women to fly military aircraft is what excites me. Imagine! I'll be able to tell my kids about flying a bomber or being the first to test-fly a new trainer plane."

"I blame myself," I admit. "Pa could have glided in for a landing without power. He had done it before. But he didn't want to take that chance with me up there with him. I guess I'm here because I owe it to him to learn how to fly. Because that should not have been his last flight. If I wasn't in the plane with him, he'd still be here." I roll over to my side, the tears starting to drop down on my pillowcase. "I can't talk about it anymore. Goodnight, Sadie."

I try to close my eyes, but all I can see is the gray, sterile atmosphere of a hospital lobby.

Charlotte ran up the stairs as quickly as her feet would carry her. She turned the corner and bolted down the corridor, heading for the last door on the left. When she opened it, she stopped in her tracks. I was laying there. My broken arm was wrapped in a cast, and my fractured ankle was elevated above the bed in a sling. I smiled, excited that she was here. That there was someone to talk with. She stared at me good and hard, but didn't smile back.

"You killed him," she calmly said, before turning around and running out the door.

⊹

"I can't believe you put syrup in my shampoo!" Cornelia screams from the showers the next morning.

"Well, ain't you a sweet little Southern belle this morning," Sadie calls back at her.

Cornelia storms into the bay wearing a towel. "Listen," she says, pointing her finger at me. "If you want me to say I'm sorry, then fine. I'm sorry I told everyone the truth."

"No, you're not," I say, my hands on my hips. "Listen, you and Sadie have an animosity going on between you two, and I don't want to get in the middle of it."

"Too late," Cornelia says, combing the tangles out of her hair. "You already have."

I don't feel like arguing. Even though it wasn't me who put the syrup in her hair, I knew she wouldn't let up about it. With a sigh, I leave the bay.

The days roll by quickly. I ace flight theory class, barely squeak by in engines, and move on to Morse code and meteorology. It rains for two days straight, and we're unable to fly. Not knowing what to do with ourselves, we spend most of our time studying, playing ping-pong in the rec room, or swapping stories over meals.

I can tell I'm gaining weight from all the wonderful food, and we all have healthy, glowing tans from the tough Texas sun.

One night it is so hot that Sadie suggests we drag our beds outside, where there is at least a cool, steady breeze. We sleep under the stars, dreaming and chatting about what it will be like to solo without our instructors. We wonder who they will pair us up with to buddy fly. And every time a plane flies overhead, we get excited about the opportunity to fly at night, something we won't learn how to do until the fourth month of training. Often, the conversation shifts back to the war. In Iowa, I never really had a clear picture of what was happening overseas. My only contribution was working in our family's victory garden. We had to plant our own vegetables so that the government could use the tin from canned vegetables to make something else that was needed. I never really got a clear picture of how this was helping. The canned vegetables were still on the shelves at the store. If we weren't buying them, someone else was, right? It didn't make any sense to me. But after hearing the other girls read their boyfriends' letters and talk about what the war effort is like back in their home towns, I realize that our flying is important. For the first time in my life, I feel that I'm doing something that matters.

In a few days we have our first check ride. A thick tension hangs in the air. We are nervous wrecks, constantly going over cockpit procedures and pouring our minds through hundreds of maps and diagrams of the airfield and the surrounding area. Finding your way around the sky can be a daunting experience, especially when all you have is a map, a compass, and a watch. We all know that one in three of us will probably wash out.

It stops raining the day before our check rides, giving us only one day of flight practice. I completely mess up on my rudder exercise. My dives are wobbly, as usual. I feel nervous and anxious, and when we land, Pick makes sure to point out all my errors and tells me there's no way I'm going to pass the test tomorrow.

After flight training, we're a sad-looking bay. Nobody performed wonderfully. Even Opal, the best of our group, went out too far before making her turns. We crumple into bed, barely speaking a word to each other. We're worn-out and anxious, and the thought that it may be the last night that some of us will sleep here is simply unbearable.

My stomach is queasy, but I force myself to eat a hard-boiled egg and sausage for breakfast. I skip the coffee, for fear that it will make me jittery while flying, or worse, have to use the restroom. We learned pretty quickly not to drink a lot of liquids before our flights. We go to calisthenics class and complete our physical training routines. Already, the exercises are easier than they were the first week of training, and I can tell my muscles are strengthening. I can even do chin-ups, something that seemed impossible the first few days of training.

After calisthenics, we march to the ready room and gear up for our check rides. Major Pick is in a good mood. Most likely he's pleased to be sending a few of us home.

"I feel like I'm going to vomit," Opal says, while the rest of us stand by. "I really don't want to go first."

"Can't blame you," I say. "I'm about to puke myself."

"You'll do fine," Sadie says to Opal as she helps her put on her parachute pack. "You're the best of the group. Smallest, yes, but also the best."

Cornelia rolls her eyes at Opal. "Just wait till we move on to AT-17s. Then we'll see how your little body handles big machinery," she tells her.

We're all silent as Opal heads out onto the field. Her flight is faultless. Her spins and stalls are well formed, her dives effortless, and her landing is nice and smooth. When she is done, she comes running toward us, a bright glowing smile pasted on her face. "Thank goodness! I can breathe again, at least for the next two weeks until the next one."

And then it is my turn. I clutch Sadie's rabbit's foot as I walk toward the PT-19A. Pick is already seated in the front cockpit, waiting for me. I take a deep breath and climb into the back cockpit.

I am able to recall almost every procedure except to check the fuel and oil pressure. When Pick points out that I have forgotten, I immediately check them and begin to worry that I blew it. That it is over. That I will be the first to be sent home.

But as we pull out onto the runway, Jackie Cochran's voice echoes loud and clear in my ears. *It was my heart that won. Because I wanted it.*

As I imagine Sadie and Opal and Deirdre and Jean and even Cornelia standing in the ready room, watching me, I know that I want to pass. I want to stay. I want to be here.

The clouds dance above me as I approach my first spin. I feel my body sink down into the seat as I tilt the nose of the plane up. Even though I'm in control of the plane, I'm dependent on so many other factors. Gravity. The movement of the wind. The feel of the engine. Each plane feels different than any other. That's what keeps it exciting.

My spin is perfect. I round out for the dive, which is still rather shaky, but less so than every other flight in the past.

I make the grade. Even Pick admits that my flying has improved drastically since yesterday. Said he thought for sure I would fail.

Sadie is next, and she passes with flying colors. So do Cornelia and Deirdre. We decide to head back and change for ground school. Deirdre waits behind for Jean to finish her check ride.

As we head back to the bay, we pass by the wishing well, the round stone fountain in between our bay and the mess hall.

A few trainees from one of the older classes stand around the well.

"So, tell us. Did y'all pass?" one of them yells at us.

"Ol' Pick didn't know what hit him today. He was preparing to fail us all for sure!" Sadie yells back.

And then suddenly, before we all know what is going on, the older girls run over to us. I feel myself being picked up.

"What's going on?" I ask as they grab my backpack and toss it on the ground.

"Tradition," one of the girls answers and then giggles. Someone is ringing the cowbell, and before I know it, every inch of me is soaked.

I look around. We are in the middle of the wishing well. Sadie, Opal, and Cornelia are also standing there, drenched.

With our zoot suits soaked, we have more than a little trouble climbing out of the well. Cornelia trips as she climbs out and hits the ground with a thud. We all erupt with laughter as she stands up and attempts to brush off the Texas dirt that is now caked all over her wet zoot suit. She scowls our way and turns to head back to the bay.

"That was a riot!" Opal says as we also head back to the bay.

"I don't even care that I'm drenched," I say as I wring the water out of my hair. "Cooled me down at least."

"You should see yourself, Miss Peach," Sadie yells ahead at Cornelia. "You look like an absolute mess. Hardly the Southern belle from Atlanta."

"Oh, leave me alone," Cornelia says as she swings our bay door open.

When we walk in our giggles and smalltalk come to a screeching halt. Jean sits on her bed. Her suitcase rests next to her. Deirdre sits with her arm around her.

"Oh my God, Jean," Opal exclaims.

Through tear-stained eyes, Jean looks up at us. "I washed out. Major Pickett said I didn't have what it takes to fly the Army way. I'm expected to leave by the end of the day."

"Oh Jean, I'm sorry," I say, walking over to her.

"It's worse than that," she says. "I went to the administrative building to sign some paperwork. When I asked them for the money they owe me, they said there wasn't any. Since I didn't make it till payday, they don't have to give me a dime. I don't know how I'm getting home. I don't have enough for a train ticket, and I can't ask my family. I know they don't have any to spare."

She begins to cry harder, and all of us pile onto the bed next to her, trying to comfort her. All except Cornelia, who walks over to her locker, and begins to rummage through her belongings.

"Here." She hands Jean a fifty-dollar bill. "Will this cover the train ticket?"

Jean looks up at her. "It's more than enough, but I can't take money from you."

"Take it," Cornelia replies. "You need it more than I do." She places the bill inside Jean's suitcase.

We help her pack, folding her clothes for her, and then sweep around her bed so she won't have to.

"I really wanted it," Jean says, looking me directly in the eyes. "I really wanted to pass. Now I'll probably have to go home and get a factory job or something. God, I want this stupid war to be over with. I just want everything to go back to the way it was before there was a war effort. Before everyone had to do their part. I wish I hadn't even come here."

"But then you wouldn't have met any of us," Opal says.

"Or gotten to fly military aircraft," Sadie says. "Listen, we all have things we want right now that we can't have. I want John to come home."

"I want my brother to be freed. Or at least to know where he is being kept," Deirdre says with a sigh.

"I want my family to be able to stop rationing their food." I think of Mom having to come home after a hard day's work and spend an hour in the victory garden picking vegetables to eat for dinner.

"I want Daniel to be proud of me," Opal says. "He wasn't so keen on me coming down here, to tell you the truth. It took a while to convince him I'd be okay, but he still has his reservations. Scared I'll fall out of a plane again."

"Again?" Sadie asks.

"Yep, I slipped right out of the safety belt once," Opal answers. "Banged up my elbow pretty bad."

Jean clicks her suitcase shut. "Now, don't go falling out of any more planes. Any of you." She sighs. "And I don't want to hear about any of you washing out either, you hear me?"

We all nod.

"Well, I have to go find a ride into town. The last train leaves in a couple hours." She wipes the tears away and gives us each a hug good-bye.

When she hugs Cornelia, she whispers quietly, "Thanks again. I'll pay you back, every cent."

"It's nothing," Cornelia says as she quickly breaks away from the hug.

And then Jean is gone.

CHAPTER EIGHT

The days fly by. We receive our first paychecks, a hundred and fifty dollars for the whole month. It's the most money I've had in my entire life. On Saturday Sadie and I go into town to open a bank account. Afterwards, I slip into the post office to mail the letter that has been resting in my pocket for several days now.

Dear Mom and Charlotte,

I hope this letter finds you both well. You don't have to worry about me. I'm doing just fine. Sweetwater is another world, compared to Iowa. We eat, sleep, and talk aviation from morning till night. We live in barracks, wear unbecoming, badly-fitted coveralls, sleep on metal cots, and are subject to strict military discipline, just like the male cadets. We march to ground school, flight line, and meals, singing songs just like the men, except we change the words a bit. The other girls here with me are wonderful, for the most part. I think you would like them. The food is fantastic, and I'm putting on a good amount of weight. We spend most of our days outside, and the Texas sun has proven an excellent cure for my pale complexion. You'd hardly recognize me.

I got my first paycheck today. Here is some money for you both. Please buy a few war bonds and spend the rest any way you think is best. I love you, and I'm sorry if you don't understand.

Byrd

I buy a stamp, hesitate for a moment, and then slip it in the mailbox. For a moment I regret my decision, wishing I could retrieve it.

Back at the soda shop, Sadie is looking through a fashion magazine. I pull a stool up next to her.

"I'm bored," she exclaims. "What should we do for the next couple hours? Go to a movie? Do you like Hitchcock films? *Shadow of a Doubt* is showing at the theater in a few hours."

"Deirdre and I saw it last weekend," I say, flipping through a magazine. "Besides, anything by Hitchcock scares me to death. Although Joseph Cotton was rather dashing, don't you think?"

Sadie shrugs. "I guess."

"You guess? Well, if not him, who then?"

Sadie looks up for a moment, gazing off into outer space. "Cary Grant," she says dreamily. "I must have seen *His Girl Friday* ten times in the theater. Fell in love with him over and over again. He's great in *Bringing Up Baby*, too. Have you seen that?"

I shake my head. "I never went to the movies back home," I admit. "The nearest theater was miles away, and Mom thought it was a waste of money."

"Well, I heard a rumor that *The Yellow Rose of Texas* is coming here in a couple weeks. You'll love Roy Rogers." Sadie blows a wisp of her hair out of her face. "What do you feel like doing? We could go to the swimming pool, but we don't have our suits with us. And I doubt the city of Sweetwater would be too keen on skinny-dipping. What do you think?" Sadie asks.

"Too hot to think," I answer, fanning myself.

The store manager walks over to us, crossing his arms. "Are you girls going to buy anything? If not, I'm going to have to ask you to leave."

"Oh fine, we'll go." Sadie grabs her purse and stands up. I follow her out the door, and we run smack-dab into Opal.

"There you both are! I've been looking all over for you," she exclaims.

"What's happening?" Sadie asks. "You're out of breath."

"We've got to get back to Avenger right away. *LIFE* magazine has taken over the entire base."

"What?" Sadie and I shout at the same time.

"They're doing a story on the WASP, and they want to talk with as many girls as they can. There are even photographers taking pictures! You should have seen Cornelia when she found out. She ran to the bathroom and spent at least an hour curling her hair and touching up her makeup."

When we get back to Avenger, the *LIFE* magazine photographers are all over the place, talking to girls and taking pictures left and right.

Lieutenant Andrews walks up to us and flashes us his winning smile. "You cadets get your picture taken yet?" We shake our heads. "Well then, come on. Let's get you in some AT-17s, and they can shoot their hearts out."

Cornelia runs up to us. "I heard something about AT-17s. Count me in," she says, and the four of us follow Lieutenant Andrews out on the airfield.

Sadie and I climb into the cockpits of one of the planes, and Cornelia and Opal climb into the other. The photographers snap several pictures of us in the AT-17s. They even get a few shots of us sitting on the wings of the planes.

It is absolute chaos, and I love every minute of it. The flash of the bulbs. The reporters running back and forth, from plane to plane.

"Say, where are you from, Miss?" Someone leans over toward me.

"Who, me?" I respond, squinting amongst the flashing bulbs to see who is talking to me. It is a young reporter wearing a red bowtie and a nice suit jacket.

"Yes, you." He smiles, pencil poised.

"Right outside of Des Moines, Iowa."

"Same as Amelia Earhart. Interesting." He scribbles on his pad. "And what do you believe is the most important thing about you being here at Sweetwater?"

I stare out at the flight line. At the other girls. At the planes. At the instructors. At the pandemonium of the reporters and the photographers running around, interested in why we are here and why we are pilots.

"I guess just knowing that a poor farm girl from Iowa has just as good of a chance as anyone else to be here, learning to fly the Army way."

He finishes scribbling and looks up at me. "Thank you for your time, Miss. And thank you also for doing your part," he says earnestly, extending his hand for me to shake. He walks away and onto the next girl, as the wind whips my hair back and the cameras keep on flashing.

We are so excited about the prospect of being in *LIFE* magazine that it takes us forever to get to bed. When it is lights out, we climb into our cots but are unable to fall asleep.

"I'm writing my folks tomorrow. They read *LIFE* religiously every week," Sadie says. "They're going to be so excited when they hear about the article. My father was featured in the magazine a few months back in an article about nuclear physics. And my mom was interviewed a year or so back in a feature about Southern horticulture. Imagine, all three members of a family chronicled in the greatest magazine in the world! We'll be immortalized."

"Do you think they took enough pictures?" Cornelia asks, concerned.

"For the last time, yes! You've been asking us that all night," Opal complains.

"Listen, you made sure all the reporters and photographers had the correct spelling of your name several times. I'm sure you'll be mentioned in some way," I tell Cornelia.

"Mentioned?" she says, dismayed. "I want to make the cover."

"Well, we don't always get what we want, do we?" Deirdre says, pointing over to Jean's vacant bed.

The white empty sheets glow eerily in the moonlight, silencing us.

It is our first day of buddy flying. As expected, Cornelia and I are still paired up together. Sadie and Opal are a pair. And with Jean gone, Deirdre is matched up with a girl from Bay 5, whose partner also washed out.

We are given our assignment: ferry the plane toward a neighboring town, where Lieutenant Andrews will meet us. Today I will be the one flying our plane, while Cornelia keeps a lookout for other aircraft.

I am glad to be flying with someone other than Pick, even if it is Cornelia. We're the first to take off. I check the longitude and slowly steer us toward our target landing post, just west of Avenger.

It's a clear day, with not a single cloud in the sky. Clear skies always make me nervous. I'm not sure why. The calmness seems deceptive. It makes me feel like the only person alive, and that when I land, there will be nothing left on earth.

"Can't you do a spin or dive? This is boring," Cornelia bellows from behind, reminding me that if we do land and there is nothing left, I would have to spend all of eternity with Cornelia and her complaining.

"Spins and dives aren't my style," I call back at her.

She sighs and sits back. "That's because you can't do a dive properly to save your life," she answers snidely.

I can feel the anger growing inside of me, but I suppress it. I can't take the risk of becoming unfocused, not in the air. "I enjoy cruising. I'm not a show-off like some people."

"Don't get smug with me, farm girl."

I decide to ignore her and we sit in silence for a few minutes. I go to check the radio beam to make sure the navigation is on target. Surprisingly, I notice that the oil pressure is relatively low.

"Hey Cornelia, take a look at this." I point at the gauge. She reluctantly strains her head forward to read the pressure.

"That doesn't look too good," she says, and I can hear a note of panic in her voice. "What's the temperature of the engine?"

"Pretty hot," I answer, checking the thermometer. "We're burning up a lot of oil here."

"Did they check the plane before we went up?" she asks.

"Of course. Both Pick and Andrews gave it a thorough look," I answer, watching as the oil gauge slips even lower. "Cornelia, we're approaching danger zone."

"What?" she exclaims.

I can feel the sweat starting to form around my temples. "There must be a leak." My mind races as I search for a solution. I hear a pounding noise, like the sound of a fist banging on a door. It takes me a few seconds to realize it is my own heartbeat. I know there's only one thing I can do at this point. "I think I have to force a landing," I tell her.

"Oh, my God. We're going to die," she shrieks back at me.

"Cornelia, listen to me. I need you to radio back to the base. Explain to Pick or whoever is there what's going on. And for goodness' sake, hold on tight!" I yell.

As I dive downward, looking for a place to land, oil splatters all over the windshield, making it impossible to see where we're going. I lean out the side of the cockpit to make out where we are. Suddenly, a wave of oil smacks me right in the face. I cough, trying to spit it out. I turn around to Cornelia.

"We're leaking! No time to radio back," I yell. "I can't see a thing. You have to look for me. I'm just going to coax the plane along until we reach somewhere we can land."

Cornelia stretches her head out the right side, also getting splattered by the oil. "Keep heading north!" she screams, as she spits the oil out of her mouth. "I think I see a grassy field."

"You think, or you know?" I holler back at her.

"There's a farm off in the distance. Just try not to hit any of the cattle."

We continue heading north, toward the farm. I place the flaps at twenty percent, and we begin our descent.

"You've got it!" Cornelia screams, her head still poking out the side of the plane. "Just bring her down nice and easy. That's it."

We coast along the field, and with a slight jolt and rumble, I make contact. Slowly, I bring the plane to a standstill. We sit there a moment, regaining our breath, allowing our hearts to reclaim their regular rhythms.

Between deep breaths Cornelia exclaims, "Thank goodness. You didn't kill us."

"Excuse me, but an oil leak is beyond my control. Oh, just wait till I get my hands on Pick." I lift the cockpit door open and slowly stand up.

"The radio is busted," Cornelia says, trying to turn the connection on, but with no luck. She looks up. "Where are we?"

I climb out of the plane and she follows. Our faces are caked with sticky, black oil. I try to wipe it off with my sleeve, but it just spreads everywhere and gets worse.

We are in the middle of a grassy field. Wildflowers grow all around, and off in the distance a weathered wooden fence lines the field. Behind it is a slightly dilapidated farmhouse.

"Let's head toward that house and see if anyone is home," I suggest.

We walk toward the farmhouse.

"Do you think they'll have a phone?" Cornelia asks.

"By the looks of it, no. But maybe someone can give us a ride into the nearest town," I answer.

"Shhh. Do you hear that?" Cornelia asks, holding her arm out for me to stop. There is a faint rumbling, pounding noise, and when we turn around, we see a herd of Longhorn cattle, heading right toward us.

"They must have been aroused by the roar of the engine," I say.

"They're gaining on us!" Cornelia says, her voice quivering with fear.

"Run!" I scream, and with a burst of adrenalin we sprint forward. I am running faster than I ever have before. The fence is closer and closer. We reach it, and Cornelia tries to swing her leg over but fails to notice a loose string of barbed wire that runs along the fence. The wire gashes her leg. She leaps back in pain.

I reach back to her, and we manage to help each other climb over, scraping ourselves a few times, until finally we are on the other side.

We turn around. The cattle have stopped running and stand there, staring at us. And then that's when we hear the click of a shotgun loading.

"Now be quiet and don't you boys move one more inch, or I'll shoot ya," a gruff Texas accent commands.

We immediately freeze in our tracks.

"Lowell, get your keister over here! We got trouble. And bring your rifle," he yells.

"Sir—" Cornelia begins to say.

"I said, shut your trap. I've shot plenty of folks before for trespassing, and I got no problem doing the two of you in as well."

"What's happening?" a younger man asks. "I brought my rifle."

"Just some trespassers, son. Now boys, I want y'all to turn around nice and slow, you hear me? No sudden moves!"

Cornelia and I glance at each other, and then slowly turn around to face them. An old wrinkled man sporting a tattered cowboy hat and a greasy shirt aims at us with his shotgun.

When he sees us, he brings the shotgun down, and takes a step forward to get a better look. "What in the name of corn?" he exclaims. "I don't know what you see Lowell, but I see a set of knockers on each of these here fellas."

Lowell, a young man of about nineteen with an adorable baby face and ruffled brown hair, looks down at the ground, embarrassed. His lips form a shy smile. "They're girls, Pa. Just a bunch of girls."

Cornelia steps forward. "Just a bunch of girls whose plane had an oil leak and had to force an emergency landing, and then were chased by a herd of Longhorn cattle, cut up by your barbed wire fence, and then held at gunpoint for trespassing."

"Sounds like you've had a busy morning so far," Lowell says, looking up at her. "And it's not even lunchtime." He smiles again. "Please, let me offer you our apologies."

"I just don't understand," the older man says, staring out at the airplane parked in his field. "Who flew the plane?"

"We did," I answer.

"No, I don't mean who was in the plane. I mean, who managed all the controls?" he sputters, unable to understand.

"We did," I answer again, but he scratches his head, still confused.

"Ignore him," Lowell says. "Are you girls hungry?"

"No," I answer. "We just need to get to a teleph—"

"I'm starving!" Cornelia suddenly interjects, and then elbows me in my gut.

Lowell's face lights up with another smile. "Well then, I'll just go whip some grub up for y'all."

Lowell gives us each a wet rag to wash up with. We manage to rub most of the oil stains off our face, but our hair is still coated with a thick layer. Cornelia's leg is pretty badly cut. Lowell ties a cloth around it to stop the bleeding.

Then he takes us to the kitchen, where we sit down at an old, splintered table. The gruff old man, Lowell's father, is named Owen, and he sits at the table with us while Lowell stands at the old metal stove, cooking.

"You girls better get that plane off my property by morning, you hear?" Owen says, chewing on a toothpick. "My cattle are having heart attacks out there, and I got a buyer coming up in a couple days. Don't want them spooked out when he gets here."

"We just need to get to a phone," I tell him.

"I'll take them into town, Pa," Lowell says. "Don't you worry."

"I know this sounds dense of me, but where are we, exactly?" Cornelia asks.

"Town of Capitola," Owen replies. "Population fifty-six. Lowell here was number forty-nine."

"Wow, and I thought Sweetwater was small," Cornelia replies.

"Capitola is proof that not everything is big in Texas," Lowell says, setting a plate of eggs and toast in front of each of us.

"Is this the last of our egg ration for the month? You know we have no food ration stamps left!" Owen declares, looking down at our plates.

"Well, what was I supposed to give them, chicken feed?"

"Toast would have been just fine. This one's not even hungry," he says, gesturing toward me.

"You can have my eggs if you want them," Cornelia says, holding her plate over toward Owen. "I don't want to take your last ones."

"Don't be silly," Lowell says, sitting down next to her. "Besides, it's not every day I get to cook for two war heroes." Lowell steals a glance at his father, who shifts uncomfortably in his seat. Lowell quickly looks back at Cornelia. "You eat them. And then we'll go into town, okay?"

Cornelia nods, and I swear her cheeks turn a shade of pink that for once is not the result of her makeup compact.

CHAPTER NINE

On the ride into town, we learn that both of Lowell's older brothers had enlisted to fight for their country. They both died within a month of each other last year.

"I wanted to enlist," he tells us as his truck turns down Capitola's Main Street. "But Pa needs me. He can't take care of the farm by himself. The past ten years have been hard on him. Ma came down with diphtheria eight years ago during the Depression, and we didn't have the money to buy her medicine. And then Ron and Benny went into the Army, hoping to make enough money to send me to school. But they didn't make it, either. I'm the only family he's got left. I just couldn't leave him."

Cornelia's eyes cloud over with a sadness I have not seen before. "My brother died in combat overseas," she says with a shaky voice. "I know how tough it must be for you and your dad. Losing one brother is hard enough, but I can't imagine losing two." Lowell turns and looks down at her. I had no idea Cornelia's brother had died in the war. Suddenly, I feel guilt-ridden.

A few hours later, Lieutenant Andrews arrives with two mechanics. While they get to work patching up the gap in the plane's oil tank, Owen looks worriedly over at his shed, where he has managed to move his entire herd of Longhorns. Every few minutes or so, there's a banging sound, then the shed shakes, and Owen gets all nervous, telling us to hurry it up, that the cattle are too riled up in there.

Lieutenant Andrews keeps apologizing to everyone, taking full responsibility for the tear, which I thought was admirable. Cornelia and Lowell sit off to the side, lost in conversation, paying absolutely no attention to what is going on around them.

When the plane is fixed, Lowell offers to give us both a ride back to Avenger. Cornelia accepts right away. I thank him profusely, but admit that Lieutenant Andrews already asked if I wanted to fly the plane back to Sweetwater with him.

Before we head back, Cornelia takes my arm and leads me over to the side of the farmhouse. "Listen," she tells me. "I don't want you going back and blabbing to everyone about my brother's death. It doesn't change anything. Understand?" Our eyes meet and I slowly nod. "Good." She looks away and walks back over toward Lowell. I watch as he helps her climb into his rusty orange pickup truck.

"Interesting combination," Lieutenant Andrews says, walking up behind me. "The Wilkins Drug heiress with a dirt-poor farm boy."

"She seems completely different around him," I admit, watching their truck kick up a good amount of dirt as it turns onto the road.

Owen storms over to us. "No dilly-dallying. I need you to get that contraption off my property." He gestures toward the plane. "And quickly! My cattle are about to bust through that door any minute." He looks nervously over at the shed.

"Again, I apologize for the inconvenience. I'll have one of the cooks whip up a turkey dinner, and I'll bring it by later in the week for you and your boy, Lieutenant Andrews tells him, and then turns toward me. "Well, Byrdie, are you ready to take her up again?"

"Yes, Sir," I answer as I look out at the plane, all silver and glimmering in the hot Texas sun.

"Please, call me Noah," he says, glancing down at me. I smile at him, but then quickly look away. I will not fall under his spell, I tell myself. I don't care how blue his eyes are.

When we land back at Avenger, everyone is waiting for us out at the airfield. When I climb down from the plane, Sadie and Opal run out to greet me.

"Are you okay?" Sadie asks, hugging me.

"We were so worried," Opal says.

"I'm fine," I assure them.

"What happened to your hair?" Sadie examines the oil sludge on top of my head.

As we head back to the bays, I explain what happened.

"Wow! I would give anything to have to make an emergency landing in the middle of nowhere. How exhilarating!" Sadie says.

"You should have seen Pick," Opal exclaims. "When you guys didn't come back in time, he was pacing around. He thought for sure you had crashed. We were all thinking the worst."

"We were lucky," I say as I take a deep breath, trying hard not to think about the worst that could have happened.

"Did you see Miss Peach when she got back? What a sight. I wish I had a camera. She had oil everywhere," Sadie says chuckling.

I want to tell her to be quiet. To stop teasing Cornelia. That she had a brother who died overseas. But I promised I wouldn't say anything. I swing the door of our bay open and brush past Sadie.

"Well, I have oil everywhere, too, so I'm going to hit the shower before it seeps into my brain."

"Don't want that," Opal replies. "Tomorrow we fly AT-17s!"

Pick doesn't say anything to Cornelia and me the next day, but I can tell he's nervous. He is more unpleasant than ever, assuring us that none of us have what it takes to fly the AT-17, that women can't maneuver such big aircraft.

He takes us up one at a time. Deirdre is first.

Back in the ready room, Cornelia cannot stop talking about Lowell.

"When he said goodnight, he leaned over to kiss my cheek, but I still had oil all over me," she tells me. "I was embarrassed at first, but then we both started laughing. Gosh, it was funny. Felt good to laugh, you know?"

Sadie leans over toward me, whispering, "I don't know who is more annoying, the old Miss Peach or the new one." I nod, but I feel sick to my stomach. Cornelia glances over at me and our eyes lock.

"Anyway," she says, her tone shifting back to one of worry and resentment. "It's my turn. Better get out there." ·

Cornelia's flight is different than all of her flights before. She's not showing off, and I can tell her heart is in it, the way she dives and pulls up. It's the closest to perfect flying I've seen from anyone yet. Major Pick agrees.

"You finally managed to get your head out of the clouds and fly the Army way, without any of your fancy spins or twists," he tells her after she lands. "You flew just as good as General Doolittle did when he raided Tokyo," Pick tells her.

"I'll fly anything," Cornelia says, smiling. "Bombers. Trainers. Pursuits. If it has a propeller, I'll give it a whirl."

"That's the spirit," Pick says, patting her on the back. Then he looks over at me. "You, Miss Bernadette Thompson, are another story. Since week one, you've failed to perform well on your dives. I'm just going to be honest. You stink at dives, kid."

I wince and stare at the ground. My face is burning with embarrassment. Everyone is listening, even the girls from Bay 5. Even Lieutenant Andrews. Why couldn't Pick have pulled me aside to talk? This wasn't fair.

"Now, I don't know what's holding you back, but you better fix it," he tells me in a stern voice. "If you can't do three perfect dives in your next check ride, I'm afraid I'll have to send you home. I've given you enough chances already. There's no reason for you not to be performing as well as the others are. You understand me?"

I nod, and then he walks off, leaving me standing there with all eyes on me. The anger burns inside and I truly feel what it's like to hate. Not Pick. Him I merely dislike. I hate myself. I hate Pa. I hate Mom and Charlotte. And Iowa. I hate who I am, and where I came from. And when Sadie leans over to put her arm around me, I hate her for having two parents. And a college education. And a boyfriend who loves her. And for always being able to say what is on her mind.

"Don't worry, Byrdie. We'll help you," she says. "You just tense up too much."

"It's no use," I say as I back away from everyone. "I don't have what it takes to fly the Army way. I don't think I belong here." It's the first time I've ever said what is on my mind out loud. I turn and walk away from them.

"She's just scared," Sadie tells the others. "She doesn't believe in herself."

"Let me talk to her," Cornelia says.

"I think I should be the one. She trusts me," Sadie answers. "Besides, Miss Peach, you don't know the first thing about what she went through when she was little."

"You mean her father? And the crash? I know more than you realize. I listen. I hear what you say to each other. What you say about me. She and I have more in common than either of you realize," Cornelia snaps back.

I walk around aimlessly, skipping both ground school and lunch. I'm not even hungry, just angry and upset. Humiliated and defeated.

The sound of footsteps approaching makes me stop in my tracks. I turn around. It's Cornelia.

"I used to be horrible at dives," she tells me. "Please let me help. We can go over all the maneuvers tonight, and Lieutenant Andrews has given me permission to take a plane up early tomorrow morning before breakfast so you can practice."

"I thought you wanted to see me sent home," I tell her. "I thought you hated me. Why do you want to help me?" I raise my voice, almost to a yell.

She sighs, and sits down on the nearest bench, right outside the rec room. "I don't entirely hate you, Byrdie."

"Then what is it?" I ask, confused.

"I..." she mutters. "I envy you."

"Envy?" I was not expecting her to say that.

"You're ordinary. And normal. I would give anything to walk in your shoes. Literally." She sighs and I can tell this is not easy for her. "I don't know why, but ever since meeting Lowell I can't stand who I am. The little rich girl whose father owns a pharmaceutical conglomerate. It embarrasses me. It's not that easy being rich. My parents, my grandparents, countless aunts and uncles, and cousins all watch me carefully, expecting me to always do the right thing. And they determine what that is. To them, flying is not the right thing to be doing with my life. They don't approve of me being here. Especially after what happened to Royal."

"You're brother?" I ask.

She nods. "After he died, they became overly protective of me. They began making plans for me to marry a friend of theirs' son. A very wealthy man, who is going to inherit an even more enormous fortune one day. They wanted to make sure I'd be taken care of. But I didn't love him. And I was still heartbroken about my brother." She chokes up a little, and looks off toward the hanger. "He was a pilot. His plane was shot down over the Pacific Northwest. He taught me how to fly. He's the only person who's ever understood me. And when I fly I feel close to him. He's up there, in Heaven, and the only way I know how to reach him is in a plane."

Time seems to stop still for a moment, as we sit there in silence. Suddenly, I feel selfish. All this time I had thought I was alone. That nobody knew what the pain was like. That I was the only one who flew in order to be closer to someone they had lost.

"Cornelia, I feel just awful about the way you've been treated. By Sadie and the others, myself included. I'm so sorry."

"Thanks. I haven't exactly been a saint myself. But I'm glad you're here. And I'm glad we're partners."

We stare up at the sky as an AT-17 does spins in the distance. It rounds out into a dive, swooping down and up into another spin.

"I really don't want to see you go home," Cornelia says in an almost whisper. "I want to help. You're the closest thing I have to an actual friend down here."

A warm feeling runs through my body. She's not that bad, I think, as we sit there watching the planes dance above us in the clear blue sky.

The next day, Cornelia pulls me out of bed at four o'clock. The mornings have grown icy cold with the arrival of fall, and I shiver as my feet hit the chilly floor. We don't even take time to shower. Instead, we change into our zoot suits and flight gear and slip out of the bay as quickly and quietly as possible.

The wind whips our faces. As we walk out onto the airfield, I can feel my nose and lips beginning to chap. Bundled up in his flight jacket, Lieutenant Andrews waits for us beside a B-25.

"Thank you so much for doing this for us, Sir," I tell him as we approach.

"I'd hate to see you go home, cadet. You've got a good team on your side, and I'm just happy to be a part of it. We all believe in you. You just have to believe in yourself."

"That's what I'm going to try to do from now on," I tell him.

"Good. We need you around here. More than you know. After all, you're the only one who can catch a snake." He winks at me and opens the cockpit door for us. "Now, let's see some winning dives."

When we reach cruising altitude, Cornelia leans forward. "Airfield is clear. Now bring her into a 180-degree turn for the setup," she says.

I whirl the B-25 into a 180-degree turn as the wind whips rapidly past us.

"Now, bring the nose up to an altitude where your feet are on the horizon," Cornelia shouts at me. This is always the hardest part for me. I always tense up and break the dive too soon, creating the shaky movement that I have become famous for. "Take your time," she calmly tells me. "I know you can do this."

Pa was an ace at dives. He could do them in his sleep if he had to. He never feared anything, had no reservations about his performance at all. I remember sitting on the grass below our house, watching his little Cub flying above me. His dives and spins were flawless. His figure-eights were as smooth as a dancing ballerina. The three of us—Mom, Charlotte, and I—would sit there together, with the rumble of Pa's engine far above us. That's the happiest I remember us all being.

There was an ever-present feeling of peace surrounding us. We were a family back then.

I need you now, Pa, I silently tell him. I need you to take away all the fear. I need to uncover the peace inside of me. I know it's there. You gave it to me. Please, help me find it.

I bring the nose of the aircraft up, and even though we hang there for only a few seconds, it feels like an eternity. I watch the tip of the plane, pointing directly up at the sky above us, and it is the most beautiful thing I have ever seen. I feel like we are about to fly through the hemisphere and right into space. The fear melts away and for once in my life, I feel completely limitless.

"Perfect!" Cornelia shouts behind me. "Now apply back-stick pressure, and when the dive breaks, center the stick and let the plane build enough airspeed so that recovery can be made smoothly without losing too much altitude."

My stomach begins to tense up as my breath falls to the pit of my belly. This usually happens, and then my hands get slippery on the controls, which causes me to shake.

"Trust the air around you," Cornelia calmly says.

I apply back-stick pressure and like children at an amusement park ride, we float downwards. The tension melts away as the plane's vibrations run through my blood, my bones, my nerves. I grab the stick, and at exactly the right moment, bring it back into the center. With a smoothness I've never been able to obtain, we move upward and into recovery.

"You did it!" Cornelia exclaims.

"It was easy. I had no idea," I tell her. I can feel the smile glowing on my face. "I just had to wait a little bit longer before centering. I just had to wait till it felt right."

"The plane will let you know when to recover. It's all about control," she says.

"The fear of falling always tenses me up, but I wasn't even scared. The fear just melted away."

"Because you believed in yourself. Now, do it again!"

I lift the tip of the plane up once again. I wait, watching the sky directly above us. *Thank you, Pa,* I tell him. I bring us back down and center the stick flawlessly, and then we cruise forward toward the purple and orange sunset creeping up above the horizon off in the distance.

CHAPTER TEN

"Must be something in the water, Thompson, because I am utterly shocked and amazed that you were able to dive like that," Pick tells me after we land from my check ride a few days later.

"So do I pass?" I ask, unable to hide the wide smile slowly creeping its way onto my face.

He scratches his head. "Unfortunately, you do," he says, looking down at me and shaking his head. He folds his arms. "I must have said something to you that finally registered in that head of yours."

"Yes, Sir. You really helped me out. Couldn't have done it without you," I tell him, rolling my eyes at Sadie, Opal, and Cornelia, who are standing in the ready room, grinning at me.

"I knew I was good, I just didn't know I was this good," Pick says. "I'm going to have a little chat with Cochran about my ranking. The way I see things, it's about time I made Colonel."

Pick actually cracks a smile before he turns and walks back toward the airfield to take the next girl up. I join the others in the ready room.

"You did it!" Sadie exclaims, hugging me.

"Of course she did," Cornelia says. "She knows she belongs here."

"I am about to burst," Opal cries out. "Can I tell her?" she asks the others.

"What is it?" I ask.

"We have the most exciting news to tell you! We didn't want to tell you earlier because you had to focus on flying, but oh, it's the best thing in the world!"

"What is it? Tell me!" I say.

"We're going to Dallas this weekend!" she shrieks. "Well, all of us except poor Deirdre. She has too many demerits and can't leave the base."

"John will be there," Sadie explains. "I just got word this morning that they're shipping him back this week. He's flying into Dallas and staying there for two days before he gets his next assignment."

"Sadie, that's wonderful!" I tell her. "How are we getting to Dallas?"

"Lowell is driving us," Cornelia says.

"Wait a minute." I look at Sadie and then at Cornelia. "What's going on? You two aren't arguing."

"It was Miss Peach's idea, actually." Sadie looks over at Cornelia, and I cannot believe what I am seeing. She's actually smiling.

"I told her all about Royal," Cornelia admits.

"And I feel just awful," Sadie says. "I wish I could wash my own mouth out with soap."

"We're not friends or anything," Cornelia is quick to say, and Sadie nods in agreement. "I just felt it would be nice to get away for a weekend. Even if it does mean we have to be around each other. Plus, I'm dying to show Lowell life outside of Capitola. Oh, I'm going to have to get him something suitable to wear for the dance, won't I?"

"Dance?" I ask. "Nobody said anything about a dance."

"John has invited us to the Governor's Ball," Sadie explains.

"What?" Cornelia exclaims. "I didn't know it was the Governor's Ball. I thought it was just a small servicemen's dance."

"Nope, it's the Governor's Ball. Isn't that exciting!" Sadie says.

"No!" Cornelia answers. "Not at all. It's dreadful."

"Why?" I ask her.

"I'm going to know everyone," Cornelia says. "My parents are friends with everyone, and they're all going to be there. I just know it."

"So?" Sadie says.

"Now I have to teach Lowell how to dance. All he's ever done is square dance. Oh, brother! And I've only got two days. Perhaps Lieutenant Andrews will give me a ride to Capitola. I've got to run. I'll see you girls at dinner." Cornelia sprints off toward the neighboring ready room to find Lieutenant Andrews.

"So, John's not going back into combat?" I ask Sadie.

She shakes her head, a look of elated relief all over her face. "He'll be assigned to a position here, on the home front. He says things are really looking up for us over there. Says they've been sending lots of fellas back home."

"That gives me hope that Daniel will be coming home soon," Opal says.

"Are you girls going to keep flying after your boys are back?" I ask them.

They both take a moment to think about this. "Of course," Sadie says. "I just love state competitions, you know? The thrill of pushing to be the best. I'm sure I'll do that some more. John's very supportive of my flying. In a few years, I want to try to race in the Bendix. The one that Cochran won."

"Daniel and I always talked about having a big family," Opal says, dreamily, "At least four, maybe five children. I love being here and flying these planes, and I'm so glad I'm doing my part for the war effort, but I think ultimately Daniel and I want to get married and open a medical practice in San Francisco, and raise a family. Daniel has a few relatives out there, and I've always wanted to go to California."

"And you?" Sadie asks me.

"I don't have a fella, remember?" I say. "Besides, I try not to think about the future too much."

"Hey, maybe you'll meet someone in Dallas!" Opal says.

"We'll see," I tell them, and then glance down at my grungy old zoot suit. "I guess I should buy a nice dress for the dance, shouldn't I?" I ask them. "Now that I have a little money in my pocket."

Immediately, they both nod their heads. "A blue one, perhaps. Or yellow," Opal says, as she leans her head to one side and tries to imagine what those colors would look like on me.

"We'll go into town this evening," Sadie says.

We hitch a ride from an upperclassman and are dropped off right in front of Sears and Roebuck. I stare up at the brick building, with its gold letters inscribed on the outside marquee. I realize that it has been years since I've been inside a department store.

When I was really little, before Pa died and when we had more money, the family used to drive to the J.C. Penney in Des Moines to shop for Easter dresses and shoes. The experience was never a pleasant one. Mom always forced me to try on practically every dress in the store before she found the perfect one. I hated it. Charlotte, on the other hand, absolutely loved to shop. She would pose in front of the full-length mirrors, admiring her reflection and how pretty she looked in every dress. I wonder how she's doing. If she's still working with Mom at the Red Cross. If she's met the man of her dreams. As I stare at the racks of dresses, a pang of sadness overcomes me.

"This one is nice," Opal says, breaking my concentration. I look over at her. She holds up a long blue dress with white flowers embroidered all over it.

I wrinkle my nose. "Too puffy and blue."

"This one's to die for!" Sadie says, holding up a slender gold rayon dress with a matching jacket. "I think I saw this modeled in *Redbook* magazine last month."

I shake my head. "Far too glamorous for my taste." I continue to scan the racks, but nothing is right. The dresses are either too plain or too gaudy, nothing in between.

I sigh, knowing I probably wouldn't find anything. Just like I was never able to find the perfect dress when I was little. If Charlotte were here, she'd know immediately which ones I should try on. Suddenly I realize that I miss my sister. And then I see it. On the other side of the room.

It is a dazzling purple satin dress that buttons down the front. A yellow raffia belt cinches the waist, causing the skirt to flare out just down to mid-calf. I walk over to it.

"Mom had one just like it when I was little," I whisper to nobody in particular as I run my fingers over the smooth fabric. Opal and Sadie walk up behind me. "She and Pa would get dressed up to go play Bunco with several of the other pilots Pa knew and their wives. She wore a dress just like this one of those times. She looked so elegant and carefree back then."

"Well, I think it's just lovely," Opal says, admiring the fabric. "Go try it on."

"I've got a darling pearl necklace that would look perfect with it. And we'll definitely have to pin your hair up," Sadie says, examining me.

"Enough about me," I tell them, a little self-conscious from all the attention. "You're the one who's going to see John for the first time in over a year. You'll need a new ensemble as well."

Sadie holds up the gaudy gold dress with the matching jacket. "When I said I liked this, I meant for me, not you."

"And I've got a red rayon dress that I brought from home that I think I'll wear. I just need to steam the wrinkles out first. It's been sitting at the bottom of my locker all this time," Opal says.

Lowell picks us up bright and early Saturday morning. Cornelia hops in the front seat of his orange pickup truck, while Sadie, Opal, and I all pile into the back of the wagon.

It's about a four-hour drive to Dallas. Although the weather is turning cold and it's rather frigid out, the sun shines high in the sky above, just bright enough to turn all of our cheeks a deep shade of pink.

"I can feel the freckles creeping their way across my nose," Sadie says, glaring up at the sun. "It's not fair. Cornelia doesn't have to endure this awful sun. Bet it's nice and shady up there." She looks into the window.

"Oh, leave her alone," I say. "You both promised you'd tolerate the other. Besides, if it wasn't for her, we wouldn't have a ride."

Sadie sighs and sits back. We ride in silence. I eventually stretch out, prop my suitcase on the floor, and rest my head against it. And like a lullaby, the truck's grumbling engine lulls me to sleep.

When I raise my head, instead of flat prairie land, there are tall buildings in the distance. I see skyscrapers, business marquees, and factories with smoke pouring out of the tall chimneys stacked along the top of the roofs.

"I've never seen buildings like these," I exclaim as we exit off the highway and begin our drive through the downtown area. "Have you been to Dallas before, Sadie?"

"Once, when I was little. My father received a physics award from Southern Methodist University, and our whole family drove down for the ceremony. I remember he gave a speech about how the 1940s would be filled with ground-breaking discoveries and that—"

Suddenly her eyes widen and she abruptly stops talking mid-sentence. "Stop the truck," she demands, pounding on the front seat window. "Stop the truck!" She pounds harder.

Lowell pulls over to the side of the street. Sadie quickly jumps to her feet, and hops over the side and onto the pavement.

"John!" she screams, running toward the figures of three men walking down the sidewalk in the distance. "John!"

One of the men turns around and sees her running toward him.

"Sadie!" he screams, and runs toward her, his arms outstretched. They collide, fitting together like two puzzle pieces, and share a kiss.

We enter the ballroom of the Adolphus Hotel at around seven that evening. The lights are dazzling, reflecting off the many chandeliers that drape down from the ornate ceiling above us. A thirty-piece brass band sits against the far wall, playing a big band swing song while men in uniform and women wearing elegant dresses dance together on the floor.

Sadie and John are inseparable, holding hands, laughing, and swapping stories. I've never seen Sadie so alive. Her cheeks are glowing, her eyes are sparkling, her auburn hair shimmers against her gold dress, and her smile illuminates her pearly-white teeth.

She and John head to the dance floor and join the other couples in a slow dance, while Opal and I head to the refreshments table to grab some punch and nibble at the vegetable platter. Across the room, Cornelia and Lowell leisurely stroll in. Lowell looks quite striking in the brand new suit that Cornelia bought him. His hair is slicked to one side, and hardly anything remains of the poor farm boy from Capitola. Cornelia is wearing a gorgeous white dress, her blond hair falling in perfect curls around her shoulders. She looks around, cautiously scanning the room, watching everyone carefully. When she spots us, she waves, and she and Lowell head over our way.

"I'm panicky as can be," she says, and then turns to Lowell. "Feel my hands, they're all clammy. I'm scared to death that I'm going to run into someone my parents know."

"Ain't Cornelia pretty when she's nervous?" Lowell says, taking her hand in his, trying to calm her down. "There's nothing to be afraid of, darlin.' Now, I say we get out there and practice some of those dance moves you taught me."

Cornelia blushes but before she can answer, an elderly woman saunters up to us. She is heavyset, and the purple dress and matching jacket she has squeezed herself into accentuates every roll of fat on her body. Her gray hair is pulled tightly into a bun on top of her head.

"Miss Wilkins, I had no idea you would be here," she shrieks at Cornelia in a high-pitched Southern drawl. "Harold, come over here. Look who it is."

Harold, an elderly man wearing a refined suit, turns away from the group of people he is mingling with.

"Miss Wilkins! What a pleasure to see you," he says as he shakes her hand.

"It is good to see you too, Mr. and Mrs. Fairbanks," Cornelia says, her mouth forming an awkward, uneasy smile. "How are you this evening?"

"Just lovely, dear," Mrs. Fairbanks says warmly. "You must have come down here with your parents, didn't you? Now, where are they?" She looks around the room. "I just must say hello."

"I'm afraid they didn't make it down. I'm actually here with some of my friends," Cornelia replies. "We drove in from Sweetwater."

"Sweetwater? Where in heaven's name is that?"

"It's four hours west of Dallas, Mrs. Fairbanks."

"What in heaven's name are you doing there?"

"I'm training for the Women's Air Force," Cornelia answers, expressionless.

"I am so confused," Mrs. Fairbanks replies. "I thought you were attending a lady's college in Nova Scotia."

"Oh. I see," Cornelia says. "I'm afraid that isn't true, Mrs. Fairbanks. Perhaps next time you see my parents, you could ask them for once to tell everyone the truth. It was good to see you both. Enjoy your evening," Cornelia says, slipping her arm into Lowell's as she walks away.

"What in heaven's name was that about?" Mrs. Fairbanks asks her husband. "Did she say something about women pilots in the Army? That's preposterous. I've never heard of such a thing."

"Perhaps the young girl has been tasting the wine this evening," Mr. Fairbanks says, watching as Cornelia and Lowell make their way toward the dance floor.

"Poor Cornelia! That was her nightmare coming true," Opal says to me, as we watch Mr. and Mrs. Fairbanks join a group of their friends.

"Excuse me, ladies," a male voice says, and we both turn around. A man wearing a military uniform stands in front of us. "I have been watching both of you pretty girls from across the room, and I noticed you both lack male companionship. I wanted to fix that for you."

"No need," Opal says, waving her hand at him. "I'm already spoken for."

"And you, Miss?" he says, turning to look down at me.

Before I can answer, Opal grabs her purse off the refreshment table. "Would you excuse me Byrdie? I'm going to go freshen up in the ladies' room," she says, giving me a small smile, and before I can protest, she saunters away.

"Byrdie. That your name?" the man asks.

I nod.

"My name is Peter Thurman, and I'm a United States Air Force pilot, and tomorrow night I'm being shipped out overseas to fly in combat," he says, batting his brown eyes down my way. "I may never come back, but if I could have just one goodbye kiss from such a breathtaking beauty as yourself, it would make the trip easier to bear. You'd be doing your country a big service."

I stand there, utterly in shock, unable to speak.

"She's already doing her country a big service, boy," a booming voice behind me says. I turn around. It is Lieutenant Andrews. "If you don't turn and walk away right now, I'll report you to your commanding officer and give you ten demerits for indecent behavior toward a fellow cadet."

"I wasn't talking to you, Sir," Peter says. "You can't write me up for squat."

"No, but I can," I answer, smiling smugly at him. "Allow me to formally introduce myself. I'm Bernadette Thompson, current trainee of the Women Air Force Service Pilots."

"Women pilots!" Peter declares with a snort. "That's baloney." He looks down at me, laughing. "A woman couldn't tell a propeller from a hole in the wall."

"What's baloney is your attitude, son," Lieutenant Andrews says. "Now, as a higher-ranking officer, I order you to leave right this minute."

"I don't understand—"

"A thousand women are ferrying planes, towing targets for gunnery practice, and flying aircraft that your fellow male pilots won't touch. For you to belittle these women's achievements is a disgrace to your country. You might as well be flying for the other side. Now, get out of my sight," Lieutenant Andrews says, staring him right in the eye.

Peter looks shaky, and when he opens his mouth, only a stammer comes out. "I—I—I—"

"That's a command, son. Now!"

Alarmed, Peter hurries off toward the main entrance.

"That was completely unnecessary, but thank you anyway, Sir," I say, helping myself to another glass of punch.

"That type of mentality is what's wrong with this country. You girls are doing everything the men are doing, yet you don't receive the same respect."

"I understand that and I agree, but you really didn't have to come to my rescue. I'm quite capable of handling things on my own," I tell him. I can feel my face beginning to burn, and suddenly my hands are all sweaty.

"Then let me make it up to you. I'm a lousy dancer. I'll let you dance with me for one song, and you can laugh all you want afterwards." He stares down at me, his attractive smile slowly creeping across his face, catching me off guard.

"What are you doing here, anyway?" I stammer.

"The governor invited me. I taught his boy how to fly a Cessna aircraft carrier years ago. So how about that dance?"

"You really want to dance with me?"

He nods and takes a step toward me. "Very much so." He extends his hand out for me to take. My heart races a million beats per second. Hesitantly, I bring my hand up and allow him to take it. We walk together toward the dance floor as the brass band begins to play a slow, romantic song. A beautiful woman wearing a long red glittery gown takes the microphone and begins singing,

So, kiss me once. And kiss me twice. And kiss me once again. It's been a long, long time.

Lieutenant Andrews slides one hand around the base of my back and gently holds my hand with the other. We're closer than we've ever been, and I silently thank Sadie for letting me borrow her deodorant earlier.

"You lied to me, Sir. Your dancing is quite impressive," I say, staring at his hand holding mine.

"I will admit that I might have had ulterior motives. And please, call me Noah."

"I don't know if the Army would approve of me calling an instructor by his first name." I smile up at him, allowing my eyes to meet his.

"I'm not your instructor. Major Pickett is."

"Still, it seems odd." I tilt my head to one side, allowing the light from the overhead chandeliers to dance across my eyes. "With all these lovely girls to chose from, why are you dancing with little ol' me?"

He smiles back at me. "That, young lady, is a story for another night."

I look away, a tad frustrated. I bet he was dancing with me because he was afraid nobody else would. "What's that supposed to mean?" I mutter.

"It means that there's something I need to tell you, but not here, not tonight. Another time. Okay?"

The song ends, and we let go of each other. We stand there awkwardly for a long moment. "Okay?" he says again, but before I can reply, Sadie and Opal rush up to us.

"Hello, Sir," Opal says to Lieutenant Andrews. "I'm sorry to interrupt. Byrdie, Cornelia is in an awful state."

"She's locked herself in a bathroom stall and has been crying uncontrollably," Sadie says. "God knows she won't talk to me. She wants you to come right away."

"Of course." I glance up at Lieutenant Andrews. "Goodnight, Sir," I tell him, and make my way as quickly as possible out of the room.

"I don't know why I'm letting it bother me so much," Cornelia manages to say, tossing another tissue in the already overflowing wastebasket. "They lied to everyone, as if me flying is the worst thing in the world. Ladies' college in Nova Scotia!"

"It hurts, I know," I tell her, patting her shoulder. "It's not right of them to have lied like that. But you have all this amazing strength, and you're going to get through this. I know you will. You've come so far."

"And graduation is right around the corner," Sadie adds. "Listen, Miss Peach, you're a darn good flyer. I admit it. Maybe we have our differences, but I always knew you'd make it to see graduation day. You're a natural. And you love flying. So what if they're not proud of you!

Who cares what other people think? You're proud of yourself, aren't you?"

Cornelia nods, wiping the tears away.

"And Lowell's proud of you. And we're proud of you," Opal says.

"Poor Lowell. I wonder what he's doing right now," Cornelia says, grabbing another tissue.

"Probably worried as can be," I tell her.

"Either that, or tasting all the fancy food," Sadie says.

"You're right. I should compose myself and get back out there. And you, Sadie, should not be wasting your time worrying about me. You only have a few more hours left with John."

"It's not like our carriage is turning into a pumpkin at the stroke of midnight," Sadie says.

"Hey, you never know," I tell her. "We may get lucky. I bet a pumpkin moves a lot faster than that old contraption of Lowell's."

Sadie and Opal giggle, but Cornelia is far from amused.

"Watch your tongue." She glances sternly up at them, but with a smile sneaking around the corners of her mouth. "I love that old contraption."

CHAPTER ELEVEN

I hate goodbyes," Sadie says the next morning as we load up the truck with our bags. "If I had my way, I wouldn't ever have to say goodbye to anyone. I'd rather just leave. At least that way the last memory they have of me would be a real one, instead of a forced hug and a goodbye."

"You'll see him again soon," I tell her. "He's here in this country now. Safe."

"I know," she says. "It's still hard to say goodbye."

We're silent the rest of the ride. Sadie naps. Opal is engrossed in a letter she is writing to Daniel. And I sit there, staring out at the ever-changing landscape that surrounds us. Texas is so similar to Iowa, I think, as we drive along past cornfields and cattle farms.

I wonder what Mom and Charlotte would think of Texas. Charlotte would love it, I was certain. If she knew that I had attended the Governor's Ball, she would be boiling with jealousy. Part of me wishes that she had gone instead of me. That she had danced with Lieutenant Andrews and tasted all the wonderful food. I feel guilty about experiencing so much more of the world than my older sister.

We arrive at Avenger around four in the afternoon. We thank Lowell for the ride, and he and Cornelia say goodnight. Bags in tow, we head back to our bay.

"Traveling sure is exhausting," Opal says.

"I could sleep for a week," Sadie says.

"You slept the whole way home," I remind her, opening the door to our bay.

Deirdre is sitting on her bunk, writing a letter to her parents back home. "How was Dallas? Tell me everything."

"Interesting," I tell her, swinging my bag onto my bed. We tell her all about the Governor's Ball.

"I wish I could have been there."

"How was your weekend?" I ask.

"Horrid at first. Had to spend all of Saturday scrubbing the mess hall because of my demerits. But you'll never believe what I did afterwards. I got to fly at night! It was exhilarating. The way the flight line is all lit up, waiting for you to zoom down it. And the stars," she sighs, reflectively. "When the sky is all big and black around you, you feel like the only person in the world. It's truly the most peaceful feeling."

"I'm dying to fly at night," Sadie quickly pipes in. "How did you manage it?"

"Well, the girls in Bay 10 have been practicing all weekend. Because of all that rain a few weeks ago, they needed to log a few more hours in order to graduate. That's how I was able to go up. I went out to the airfield to watch them take off. They were short a girl, so I got to go up with one of them."

"Are they flying tonight?" Sadie asks.

"I believe so," Deirdre answers. "I want to go again so badly, but I haven't finished my Morse code exercises, and the last thing I need is another demerit."

"Ugh," Opal says. "That reminds me. I have a meteorology exam to study for."

"Well, I'm going out to the airfield after dinner. I've got that itch to fly tonight. And as you all know, you can't ignore that kind of itch for long," Sadie declares as she unpacks her belongings.

Dinner is a welcomed meal. We dine on meatloaf, mashed potatoes, bread, and Jell-O for dessert. I even go back for seconds.

After dinner, Deirdre and Opal head back to the bay to finish their studying while Sadie, Cornelia, and I trek out to the airfield to watch the girls in Bay 10 night fly.

Sadie gasps as a wave of euphoria spreads across her face. "They're flying B-25 bombers. I think I've died and gone to heaven. John will faint when he hears about this. He hasn't even flown one. We write to each other about them all the time. Oh, he'll be so jealous if I go up in one before he does. Just look at how big they are. The wingspan is absolutely gorgeous."

The girls from Bay 10 all wait in the ready room together while a few flight instructors, including Major Pick and Lieutenant Andrews, go over night-flight procedures with them.

It's not quite dark yet. The sun is setting off in the horizon, illuminating the sky in rich pinks and oranges, with yellow swirled in.

"That's got to be the prettiest sunset I've ever seen in my entire life," Sadie declares, staring out at it.

We sit there in silence, watching as the sun slowly sinks down, touching the edge of the world, and then gradually disappears from sight. The colors slowly vanish, and like a thief, night creeps in. Stars speckle the dark Texas sky as the moon glows above us, making the B-25s on the airfield glisten like black patent leather shoes.

The girls in Bay 10 jump into the cockpits, two for each machine. The first engine starts and takes off and then a second.

"Look at them," Sadie says, watching in awe as the propeller on the third plane begins to spin, preparing to go up. "Aren't they the most beautiful things you've ever seen? Look how the moonlight and the stars bounce the light all over them, making them glossy and polished. They're the spitting image of Edgar Allen Poe's *The Raven*."

"Oh, I absolutely detest Poe!" Cornelia declares, wrinkling her nose. "I had to read him when I attended a college preparatory school. His words are so murky and dark. Like mildew."

"I've actually never read any Poe," I admit.

"Oh, you should," Sadie says. "His words haunt you long after you read them." She stands, and looks out as two more B-25s are rolled out onto the airfield.

"'But the raven, sitting lonely on the placid bust, spoke only, That one word, as if his soul in that one word he did outpour. Nothing further than he uttered—not a feather then he fluttered—Till I scarcely more than muttered "Other friends have flown before—On the morrow will he leave me, as my hopes have flown before." Then the bird said, "Nevermore." ' " Sadie pauses a moment, and then looks over at us. "I can still hear my mother's voice in my head whenever I recite it. She used to read me Poe when I was a little girl. And I loved *The Raven* most of all. My mom said it was because I have a pilot's heart."

She pauses and looks at us. "You see, the narrator in the poem has no idea whether the raven will be there in the morning. It could just take off at any time and fly away, never to return. And nobody would know where it flew off to. But for a hundred and eight beautifully written lines, we are swept up in the mystery of why it is there and where it has been and where it is going or whether it will leave. Poe never tells us what happens in the end. It's up to us to decipher."

We sit a moment, taking in Sadie's words, staring out at the B-25s, still shiny and black. They do look like ravens, I realize.

"Hey, you!" a flight instructor yells our way, breaking our conversation. "I've got a sick pilot over here. Any of you want to clock a few hours of night flying?"

We glance at each other for a moment.

"Please, let me go," Sadie says, her eyes pleading at us to say yes.

"Of course. You should go," Cornelia says. "Just be careful. A bomber is a hard plane to maneuver."

"You've flown one before? Why didn't you tell us?" Sadie says.

"Guess my bragging days are over," Cornelia replies, smugly.

"Well, well Miss Peach, I never thought I'd live to see the day you'd say that." She looks over at me. "How about it, Byrdie? You don't mind if I'm the one to go, do you?"

"Of course not." I shake my head. "I have all of next month to master the B-25. Besides, I prefer smaller planes like Cubs and PTs. I don't think I should be trying to fly a bomber for the first time at night."

"You underestimate yourself, kid. And for no good reason, either." Sadie laughs. "Tonight, I'm thankful you do because it works in my favor. But don't think I won't be hard on you tomorrow." She grins before turning toward the instructor and waves her arm in the air. "I'll do it!" she screams over the sound of the plane's engine revving up. "Just let me suit up first." She turns to us. "I promise to tell you all about it. Every last detail. We'll stay up all night if we have to. I'll memorize every star in the sky and every light from all the houses below. It'll be like flying between two heavens, one below and one above. I just hope I remember to land on the right one."

She winks at me and then turns, sprinting toward the ready room to suit up. The instructor goes over a few night-flight procedures with her, and then she and the other pilot climb into the cockpit. Within a few minutes, they take off.

Cornelia and I sit in the dark, watching the empty airfield. Lieutenant Andrews walks up to us.

"Sure is getting cold here, isn't it? Never thought Texas was capable of getting this chilly." He sits down next to us on the ground. "In all those Westerns I read when I was a little boy, never once was there any mention of a cowboy needing a winter coat."

"Where are you from, Sir? You've never said," Cornelia asks.

"Holly Springs, Iowa," he answers, glancing over at me. "Bet you didn't know that, did you, cadet? We come from the same state."

"Really," I answer, taking a moment to absorb this information. "Do you still have family back there?"

"Yep. Parents, aunts, uncles, cousins. My sister just got married and moved to Des Moines."

"How did you start flying?" I ask.

He smiles, and then looks up at the sky. "Same way you did, actually," he answers, but before he can elaborate, one of the other flight instructors runs up to us.

"Andrews, we need you right away," he says, his voice stern.

"What is it?" Lieutenant Andrews asks, as he stands up and brushes the Texas dirt off of his trousers.

"Not here. The office in the hangar," the flight instructor says, glancing over at Cornelia and myself.

Lieutenant Andrews follows the flight instructor, and they disappear into the hanger.

"What do you think that was all about?" Cornelia asks.

I shrug. "Beats me. Say, how strange do you think it is that Lieutenant Andrews is also from Iowa?"

"Why do you ask?"

"He's being very mysterious lately, and I'm not sure what to make of it. At the dance he mentioned that he had something to tell me but couldn't at that particular moment. And just now he said he learned to fly the same way I did. What do you make of it?"

Cornelia raises one eyebrow. "Maybe he has a crush on you."

I purse my lips and quickly shake my head. "No. It's something else."

We sit in silence, and watch as one of the B-25s comes in for landing.

"Is that Sadie?" Cornelia asks.

"Can't tell yet," I answer, standing up and taking a few steps forward. The plane rides around the field for a few moments and comes to a stop right by the ready room. The cockpit doors swing open, and two girls climb out.

"Nope, definitely not Sadie," I say. I'm about to sit back down when something catches my eye. Three flight instructors, including Major Pickett, rush out to the two girls who just flew in. They spend a few minutes talking with them and then lead them into the hanger.

"Something's going on," Cornelia says, pointing above us. "Look, another one is coming in. It wasn't up there that long, either."

The second B-25 touches down and lands on the airfield. Two other girls emerge from the cockpits, and the same thing happens. The instructors rush out to meet them, spend a few minutes asking them questions, and then escort them into the hanger.

"Let's go see what's going on," I say, and we make our way toward the hanger.

One of the planes went down over a farm just south of Sweetwater. That's all we know so far. Major Pickett radioed all the pilots at once, instructing them to turn around immediately and make an emergency landing. There's no way to tell whose plane it is until everyone else is back on the ground. Process of elimination.

By now, everyone at Avenger is aware of the crash, and hundreds of girls stand on the side of the airfield, waiting together anxiously.

"This is all my fault," Deirdre says. "If I hadn't said anything about night flying, Sadie would be in our bay studying for tomorrow's exam right now."

"You can't blame yourself," I tell her. "She would have caught wind of the news at dinner and come out here anyway."

"I can't even imagine," Opal says. "If it's her…" Her words trail off as she begins to tear up. Cornelia leans over and puts her arm around her.

"Someone's coming in!" one of the girls from the other bay yells, pointing up at a small light in the distance. It's a B-25, circling around for its landing. Everyone watches with bated breath.

"Oh God, this is it. The last plane," Deirdre says. "I can't look." Turning toward me, she burrows her face in my shoulder.

We stand together in agonizing silence as the plane touches down and then circles around the airfield before coming to a final stop outside of the hanger. Time seems to stand still for several unbearable minutes before the cockpit door opens.

We see a tuft of blonde hair on top of the first girl's head as she climbs out. It's Jane Grady, one of the top pilots in Bay 10. Behind her, Claire Morgan exits the cockpit. Their relieved bay mates and friends run out to meet them, taking turns hugging and embracing them.

My eyes are clouding over. I can feel the wetness hit my cheeks, but I'm not exactly sure where it's coming from. Someone is squeezing my hand, but I can't tell who it is. I feel absolutely numb. Sadie is dead.

CHAPTER TWELVE

Just southeast of Sweetwater, right outside of Nolan, Texas, Sadie's B-25 collided in midair with a C-46, a cargo plane ferrying rubber and collected scrap metal to be recycled for the war effort. The C-46 pilot, a young male cadet, was ferrying the plane to a factory on the East Coast. His engine failed, and he lost control of his aircraft. Sadie tried to get out of the way, but it was too late. His nose hit her tailplane, and they both went down.

A nearby farmer and his young daughter found their bodies near the wreckage. The other pilot in the plane with Sadie was Gloria Hollingsworth, a trainee from Bay 10. Gloria would have graduated in less than a week.

The silence surrounds us like storm clouds rolling hastily across an angry gray sky. I look at Opal and Cornelia and Deirdre and something in their eyes has permanently changed. A heavy feeling of despair has replaced the wide-eyed wonderment that was there just a few hours ago. I feel it also, clutching at my heart, filling me with so many feelings. Feelings I never wanted to experience again. Feelings I thought were buried with Pa's body.

My mind races frantically. Maybe this is just one of my nightmares, and when I wake up Sadie will be standing over me, demanding that I get out of bed. Telling me that formation is in twenty minutes, like she did every morning. She will be there, I try to tell myself, but my eyes drop tears down onto my shirt. I am unable to swallow. And everything feels like it is in slow motion.

We're told to go back to our bays, to get a good night's sleep. We're told that tomorrow will be just another ordinary day, same as all the others. That breakfast, calisthenics, flight training, lunch, ground school, dinner, and all the rest will continue as normal. But how can everything go back to normal? None of us know.

When we reach the door of our bay, we stand outside, unable to open it and go inside.

"Her stuff's in there," Opal says, pursing her lips together, attempting to prevent them from quivering. "Her clothes. Her hair curlers. Her letters from John. Oh my goodness, John. And her parents. Can you imagine? They're all probably sound asleep right now. But they're going to wake up tomorrow, and their entire world will have changed overnight."

She collapses onto the ground. Her small body heaves uncontrollably as she sobs. I look over at Cornelia. Tears are streaming down her face.

"I can't go in there," she says. "We may not have gotten along, but I did admire her. She was brass and bold and had the courage to say anything she was thinking or feeling. I can't sleep in there tonight."

We pull our beds out of the bay, and despite the chilly wind around us, we sleep under the stars. I toss and turn all night, unable to rest. All I can think about is the first time I met Sadie on the train to Sweetwater, and how excited she was about flying military aircraft. And how strong and fearless she was.

"Do you think this is all really worth it?" I ask the others. "What happened to Sadie could happen again."

Opal looks over at me. Her eyes are still red and puffy. "I was just thinking the same thing. We're doing what is asked of us. We're helping the war effort. And even though we're not overseas like the men, it's just as dangerous. I'm not ready to die. I can't stand to think of what would happen if it were me instead. What Daniel would be going through. And my mother. She can't read English. They'd send her a telegram and she'd have to get it translated."

Cornelia sits up. "I keep wondering what exactly happened to her up there. You can't always see another aircraft when it's pitch-black. Sometimes I forget that what we're doing can be dangerous."

"I heard some of the girls who went out on assignment after training had to tow targets for gunnery practice. Imagine. Men whose job it is to shoot at you. The thought is just so unsettling," Deirdre says.

"Did you hear that two of the girls from Bay 6 went home today after the crash?" Opal says. "They just up and quit."

"I thought of quitting," Cornelia admits. "But my brother didn't quit. Neither did Lowell's brothers. If everyone quits, we're as good as dead."

We lay there, thinking about everything. Suddenly a feeling passes over me that I've never felt before. It calms my racing heart and it takes a few minutes for me to realize that it's pride. I'm proud to be here. Just as I'm proud to have known Sadie.

As I close my eyes, the words Sadie recited to us from Poe's poem ring loud and clear in my head: *"Other friends have flown before—On the morrow will he leave me, as my hopes have flown before. Then the bird said, 'Nevermore.'"*

And I realize that this was how she would have wanted to depart this life, as she put it, *"flying between two heavens, one below and one above."*

The next morning we somberly head out to the airfield, but with Sadie gone, none of us feel like flying. Even Major Pickett seems rather glum and dismisses us early. Cornelia and I spot Lieutenant Andrews pacing around in the ready room, and we head over to see if he has any more details.

"They've alerted her family," he says, as we walk back toward the hanger with him. "But there's something else I need to talk to you about. The military has refused to pay for her body to be shipped back to Oklahoma."

"What do you mean?" Cornelia exclaims.

"Can they do that?" I ask, the anger beginning to boil up inside of me.

"Because the WASP have not technically been officially militarized as of yet, the government holds no responsibility for the death of any of the trainees. It's up to the family and friends of the deceased to deal with details such as this. It's unfair, I know," Lieutenant Andrews sighs. "Cochran's been fighting in Washington for you girls to become an official division of the Air Force, but for now, it's still in an experimental phase."

"So Sadie's family not only has to mourn her death, they are also responsible for paying to ship their only child's body back to them to be buried?" My heart is on fire.

"I'll put in money," Cornelia says, without thought. "Whatever it takes. I'll steal the cattle wagon and drive her body back to Oklahoma myself if I have to. This can't be happening!"

"Listen, I've seen this happen before," Lieutenant Andrews says as he sits beside us. "At least one girl in each class meets her fate at Avenger, for various unfortunate reasons. The most important thing is that you remember Sadie in the way she would have wanted: as a very brave pilot. You keep her alive inside of you. For now, unfortunately, that's all you can do."

Cornelia and I head back to the bay and tell the others about the horrible situation. We're all distressed and sleep-deprived, but without any hesitation, everyone agrees to chip in money to help send Sadie's body back home to her parents.

"I can't believe they would do this," Opal says. "I can't believe they won't pay for her body to be sent home and give her a proper military burial. It's as if what she's done means nothing."

"The men get everything," Cornelia exclaims, throwing her arms in the air and pacing around the bay. "And what do we get? We're lucky they're letting us touch the darn planes. I mean, they're spending so much money on teaching us how to fly so the men can go overseas. We're part of an equation, nothing more."

"But it sure beats rolling bandages for the Red Cross," I say, imagining Mom and Charlotte sitting at our living room table, doing just that. "I can't imagine being anywhere else than here, with you all, being the first women to fly these ships. If Sadie could do it over again, I bet she wouldn't do anything different."

Deirdre nods and says, "When we're militarized with the rest of the Air Force, they'll know all about what we've done and all that we've accomplished, and how girls like Sadie died for their country and deserve due recognition. Her death shouldn't be any less heroic then the deaths of the boys and men who've died defending their country overseas."

"Sadie was an excellent pilot, one of the best I've ever known," I say. "She flew better than most men. And she knew it, too."

"Not to mention it was a male pilot who collided with her, and not the other way around," Cornelia says almost hatefully.

We arrange to have Sadie's body sent back to her parents in Oklahoma. We spend the rest of the afternoon packing up all of her stuff, reading her letters from John, and talking about what an amazing and strong pilot she was. Several girls from the other bays stop by to share their stories about her.

One of the girls from Bay 5, Betty Hughes, walks in, holding a rolled-up magazine in one hand. "Have you seen this week's *LIFE?*" she asks, sitting down next to Cornelia on the bed. We shake our heads.

"I just got it in the mail today. My parents sent it to me." As Betty begins to unroll the magazine, Cornelia suddenly gasps. We all pile on the bed around them, straining our necks to get a better look.

On the cover is a photograph of a girl sitting sidesaddle on the wing of an AT-6. She wears her zoot suit with the sleeves rolled up above her elbows and the waist cinched with a belt. Her eyes look up to the side, as if she's staring at the sky or at another plane coming in for a landing. She looks serious and determined, but full of life at the same time. In the left corner of the cover, the words "Air Force Pilot" are printed over the girl's photograph. It's Cornelia.

She stares down at the cover. "To tell you the truth, I had completely forgotten about our article."

"Imagine," Betty says. "Millions of Americans know who you are and what you're doing for your country."

Cornelia shakes her head as a tear begins to slip its way down her cheek. She quickly wipes it away. "I never actually thought it would be me…" Her words trail off, as she bites down on her lower lip and sighs. "It's not even that important anymore, you know?" She looks over at me. "Maybe a month ago this would have been the best thing in the world that could happen, but now, I don't know how to feel about it. I'd almost rather Sadie made the cover. Or one of you." She looks around at us.

"Oh, but everyone else is inside!" Betty exclaims. "Look here." She takes the magazine and turns to the article. We lean over, glancing through all the photographs. There's one of Opal, Sadie, and me wearing our zoot suits, standing together outside the hanger, right in front of a row of PT-17s. Our arms are slung over each other's shoulders, and I think that Sadie must have just cracked a joke before the picture was taken, because I look like I'm trying extremely hard not to laugh, and Opal's smile is extra wide.

Lieutenant Andrews' words ring true in my mind. *Keep her alive inside of you*, he had said, and as I stare down at her face in the photograph I know that's what I have to do. This isn't goodbye. Sadie didn't like goodbyes. I'd see her again soon. And I know just where to find her.

The next day we head out to flight training bright and early. But instead of Pick, Lieutenant Andrews greets us on the field, and the flutter in my heart that I've grown to dislike returns.

"Hey, what happened to Major Pick?" Opal asks, looking around.

"He had to fly out to D.C. for a few days. Military business. In the meantime, you're stuck with me." He smiles at us.

"Could be worse," Cornelia says. "At least we get to fly today. It'll take our minds off everything else."

"That's the spirit!" Lieutenant Andrews says, pointing toward a B-17. "Now, Cornelia and Opal, I need you to both take her up and clock a few more hours buddy flying. Deirdre, there's a girl from Bay 5 who needs to log a few more hours, and after I give her a demerit for being late, you two are going to take the B-26 up for a ride. Okay? Everyone clear?"

They all nod. Cornelia and Opal head toward the B-17. Deirdre heads toward the B-26 and begins to suit up and put on her parachute pack. Lieutenant Andrews and I stand there. He gazes out toward the bays, awaiting Deirdre's partner.

"What about me, Sir?" I ask him with a straight face. "Which plane am I taking up?"

He looks down at me a moment, and then points out at the airfield. "That AT-11. I'm going to teach you how to do a chandelle, which is when you swing the plane from side to side in the air. Like rocking a baby."

"I know what a chandelle is," I tell him. "Why are you bothering to teach me?"

"Because when Major Pickett gets back, that's the next thing he's got planned for y'all. And I figure if we give you a head start, he won't know what hit him. Listen, the truth of the matter is he's never had this many girls from one bay stick around this long. I know he'll be looking for any and every reason to fail one of you before graduation. I'm just making sure that doesn't happen to certain people." He winks at me, and my heart pounds. I quickly glance away, a tad embarrassed.

Suddenly, the girl from Bay 5 runs up to us. She's out of breath. "Lieutenant Andrews, Sir. I'm sorry I'm late again. I thought I saw a spider crawling into my parachute pack. I had to empty it and make sure it wasn't in there. I'm a Philadelphia girl. I'm scared to death of spiders."

"I don't want to hear it, Florence. Spider or no spider, you need to be on time for flight training. Now, get your keister up in that B-26. I don't want to give you any more demerits than I already have."

She nods and frantically runs off toward Deirdre and the B-26. Lieutenant Andrews looks over at me. "I'm not one for extreme discipline, as you know, but that one's always late, and sometimes I've got to be hard on her." His smile slowly comes back as he loses the stern sense of authority. "So are you ready to master the chandelle?" he asks.

I nod, and we both head toward the AT-11.

"To execute a chandelle, first you bank the aircraft on one side to start the turn," Lieutenant Andrews tells me. "Watch carefully." He takes hold of the front controls and brings the aircraft up to the left side. "Then you pull the stick back gently to climb while you're turning. Not too hard, though. Speed isn't what you want. It's all about the timing." He lightly pulls the stick back, and the plane slowly ascends while still turning.

"Now, center the stick and recover. Like this." He pushes the stick back to the center, while breaking the turn at the same time. We float backwards and to the right until we're perfectly straight again. "And that, my dear, is the chandelle. Now you try."

I take hold of the back controls and carefully follow his instructions. When I pull the stick back and the nose heads up, I freeze, unsure of what to do next.

"Just take your time," Lieutenant Andrews says. "Don't be nervous."

I gently push the stick back to the center and bank the plane to the right until we fully recover.

"Not bad," he says. "Now do it again."

I practice a few more times, until he feels that I've mastered it.

And then we just cruise.

I admit the curiosity is starting to build up inside of me. Ever since we've returned from Dallas, I find myself wondering quite often what he wanted to tell me at the dance. Now seems like the perfect time to ask. I take a deep breath and decide to go for it.

"Lieutenant, what was it that you wanted to tell me about at the Governor's Ball?" I ask.

With a sigh, he pauses a moment, looks over at me, smiles that smile, and then focuses back on the controls. "It's about why and how I became a pilot. You see, when I was a little boy, our family would drive every year to the State Fair in Des Moines. I remember it fondly. The smell of fried chicken and livestock. Eating cotton candy for the first time. Playing horseshoes with my older sisters. Watching pig races.

Playing games in the penny arcade with my childhood friends." He pauses, lost in thought. "Sure was fun."

"I used to go when I was little, too," I tell him. "Before Pa died, we would go as a family. He occasionally offered kids rides in his Cub for fifty cents a pop."

Lieutenant Andrews looks over at me, a gaze of sadness spreading across his face.

"What is it?" I ask him.

"Your pa used to take me up in the air with him. Getting to ride with him in his plane, that was the best part of the fair. Being so high in the sky, while everything else was far below us. It amazed me. I came back every year. Your pa, who I just called Mr. Thompson, always recognized me, even remembered my name. I was about fifteen when I stood in his line for the last time. He looked at me and said, 'Son, with all the quarters you've spent riding in this plane, I think it's about time you use your money toward getting someone to teach you how to fly yourself. You're going to look awful silly standing in this line with all the other kids when you're twenty, now won't you?' The thought to take lessons hadn't occurred to me. But it made complete sense. And he gave me my first lesson the very next day."

I sit there, aghast, almost unable to comprehend what he's telling me. I look out the side of the plane at the cotton candy clouds that surround us, and I remember what flying with Pa felt like. The way the earth looked upside-down when he practiced spins. The way the inside of my stomach felt like a roller coaster. The excitement I'd wake up with on a day I knew we'd go flying.

"He was a wonderful person, Byrdie." Lieutenant Andrews looks at me. "Just like you, I learned how to fly from the best. When I read about the plane crash, I was devastated. I couldn't attend the funeral because I was away at college at the time. But I felt for all of you. Especially you."

I smile wearily. "Of all things I've had to learn in ground school, the one thing I find myself going over and over again is what to do when the engine fails. Especially during a dive formation. I realize now that

Pa's Cub was so old that if he had tried to glide it in for a landing, it probably wouldn't have been able to handle the impact. He would have lost control. That's why we had to jump. He sacrificed his life to save mine."

"He talked about you all the time and how he was going to make sure that you'd be the best pilot of your generation, man or woman."

My eyes water and my heart soars. Suddenly, it's all clear to me. All the attention that Lieutenant Andrews has given me. When I couldn't do dives. At the dance. And right now, teaching me the chandelle. "I understand now," I tell him. "You're looking out for me. You're looking out for me for Pa."

He nods. "When I found out you were here, I told myself that I owe it to your father to make sure you graduate. I owe it to your father to be proud of you for him. Which I am, by the way."

"But why did you wait so long to tell me all of this?" I ask.

"When you arrived, you were a good pilot. But you had a lot to conquer. A lot to realize. A lot to move past. I didn't want to risk affecting your journey of becoming a great pilot. But you've done it, kid. And that's what you are right now, at this moment. You're a great pilot."

"But not the best, right?"

"Our country is at war, Byrdie. It's not about being the best anymore. Besides, how can 'the best' be measured during days like these? If a pilot destroys at least five enemy aircraft in air-to-air combat overseas, he's given the honor of becoming an Ace pilot. Is that the best? Or does winning a competition like the Bendix, like Jackie Cochran did, make someone the best? I'm not sure what determines 'the best.' I'm not sure that can even be measured. All I know is, if you do the best that you can, and not let anything stand in the way, including the fears of those who love you the most, and you succeed in accomplishing your goal, that is the true reward."

"The fears of those who love me the most? So you know about Mom and Charlotte?"

"I had a hunch."

"I haven't heard from them. Each month I send them part of my paycheck, and each day the mail comes without a letter or even a tele-gram to acknowledge they received the money."

"That must be very hard."

"At first it was, but now I understand it's because they're mad at me. I left home without saying goodbye. I miss them. More than I thought I would. And I feel guilty. Not about flying, about having this experience while they're stuck in Iowa. I know they'll never understand why I left them. But if they could only be here for a day, maybe they'd see that it's what I want."

"Have you talked to them about how you feel?"

I shake my head. "No. I can't find the right words to put in a letter. It'd be easier in person. But who knows when I'll get that opportunity."

Lieutenant Andrews doesn't respond, and we cruise in silence for the rest of our flight.

CHAPTER THIRTEEN

O ur last check ride is in the B-26, the biggest bomber at
Avenger. After graduation many of us will most likely get
jobs ferrying large bombers across the country or test-flying
brand new ships. We heard about how after the girls in Bay 10 graduated, they went on to test the Boeing B-29 "Superfortress" bomber,
America's biggest aircraft to date. Because of its size, and a rumor
about a faulty part on the assembly line, male pilots were apprehensive
about flying it. So the commanding officer had the girls from Bay 10
test the plane out, to show the boys that if girls could fly the B-29,
there was no reason that they couldn't. And it worked. The boys had
no fears after they saw a bunch of girls do the job.

We're nervous wrecks at breakfast, going over all the B-26 cockpit
procedures and pouring over maps of Avenger and the surrounding
areas. Opal even went so far as to go out and read the anemometer,
a device that measures wind movement. It's a good thing she did because, unfortunately, the freezing winds are moving rapidly today, and
we'll need to constantly be aware of that during our exercises.

With arms crossed and eyes squinting up at the sky, Pick, who has
returned from his trip, waits for us out on the airfield. In the ready
room, my stomach churns as we help each other put on our parachutes.

Cornelia goes up first. I can barely watch as her B-26 lifts up in the
air and takes off. I feel like I'm about to be sick. I sit on the bench, waiting, dreading the possibility that I might make a mistake that could
send me home.

"Let's go, Thompson!" Pick bellows at me from the airfield.

I successfully mount the B-26 into a steady takeoff, and before I know it, we are up in the air. My spins and dives are flawless. I perform three outstanding chandelles, and even Pick himself mutters that I'm doing well.

"Now bring her into a nose dive, and recover smooth and straight," Pick commands. I grab the control and steer the ship around, preparing to dive. "Hold on tight!" I tell him as I push down hard on the stick.

The plane dives downward and for a moment I have that carefree feeling—until we suddenly lurch to the right and start to shake from side to side.

"What's happening!?" I yell at Pick.

Pick frantically takes over the controls, but nothing happens. "The engine's dead!" he bellows at me. "Bring the stick up as fast as you can!"

I grab the stick with two hands and pull back on it as hard as possible. With a jolt, the plane tilts upward. I hear a resounding boom from behind me, and when I turn, to my horror, Major Pick lies unconscious, bleeding from the head. Oh, no. I brought it up too fast.

"Major Pickett, are you okay? Major! Please get up! Please! We need to jump!" I yell, but he doesn't move. My mind races with panic as we continue to lose altitude. "What do I do?" I scream, tears filling my eyes. I take a deep breath. "Calm down," I tell myself. "I just have to land. I can do this."

I check the altimeter. We're at 35,000 feet. I try to remember everything I learned in ground school about landing a plane without power. I have to somehow glide us smoothly into a landing. In order to do this, I have to make sure we're falling at the right speed. For every foot we come down, we need to move five feet forward. That's about eighty-five miles of flying, or about twenty minutes, to get back to Avenger before the altimeter reaches zero. I bring the nose up a little to slow us down a bit. Then I reach for the radio.

"This is Thompson. I have a situation at 35,000 feet. I've lost all power and need to come in for a landing immediately. Is anybody there?"

My radio crackles a little before the red light brightens, and Lieutenant Andrew's voice booms at me. "Byrdie! Listen to me, when you get to 5,000 feet, jump. Do you understand?"

"Negative, Sir. Major Pickett is unconscious and needs to get medical treatment at once. I can't leave him."

A few seconds of crackling goes by. "All right," Lieutenant Andrews says. "Now, listen to me carefully. I need you to dump the contents of your fuel tank. This'll reduce the danger of fire upon landing and decrease the weight of the plane."

I reach over to the gas controllers and slowly release all the fuel. "Okay," I tell him.

"Now just bring her down and forward, gliding as slowly as possible back toward base. I'm going to go alert traffic control that we're going to need every last inch of the runway. Just keep gliding, and I'll be back in a few minutes. Okay?"

"Yes, Lieutenant," I place the radio back down, and take a deep breath as I look out around me. Snow flurries fly past the window, and I become conscious that I haven't even noticed how cold it is. A chill runs through my bones, and I find myself wondering if there is snow on the ground in Iowa yet. And then the thought that I may never see Mom or Charlotte again wafts through my mind, and I realize that's what scares me the most.

My radio lights up. I turn it on.

"Byrdie. The runway's clear. What's your location?"

"About sixty miles north of Avenger, including altitude. I'm heading south as we speak."

"Okay," he says. "Now listen carefully—"

The icy wind suddenly jolts the plane to the side, disengaging the radio connection. Instead of Lieutenant Andrew's voice, a dead crackling noise sputters out. "Hello? Lieutenant Andrews!" I frantically scream. "Hello? Lieutenant! Noah!"

But there is no answer. I quickly turn the plane away from the wind, and in doing so, away from Avenger. "This is it," I tell myself. "This is how I'm going to die. This is how Pick will die. I don't know what to do."

I bang my head down on the controls as my heart swells with panic and tears stream down my cheeks. I look out over the right side of the plane. And that's when I remember something that I learned in meteorology class about using weather to our advantage. If I head west instead and come under the air movement from the north, I can land with the wind on my tail, instead of against it. I look at the altitude. It would be cutting it close, but I have to give it a try. I have no other option.

I lift the nose of the plane up to slow it down a bit and rotate the stick to the right, and the plane steers west. When the wind subsides, I round out in a turn and head north. I can feel the wind pushing me from behind, helping the plane move forward, and off in the distance Avenger Field's tower comes into view. I quickly push down on the stick, causing the plane to drop altitude rapidly, so I will be low enough to cruise into a landing. I look at the mileage. We're moving at sixty miles per hour. Still too fast, I think, and lift the nose up again to slow the plane down. I pass over the runway once, circling the plane around. I need to slow down further, so I dump the flaps.

I'm going forty miles per hour. The flight line is in front of me. I take a deep breath and slowly, slightly push the stick down, keeping the plane pointed straight in front. The closer I get to the runway, the faster my heart beats. Closer…closer…and with a jolt, I make contact. I grab back on the stick and pull as hard as I can, keeping a close eye on the speedometer as it decreases to thirty, and then twenty. At fifteen miles per hour, the plane hits something, probably an icy patch, whipping us into a ninety-degree turn to the left. When we come to an abrupt stop out in the airfield, my right shoulder crashes into the side of the cockpit as the seatbelt around my waist pulls me back. And then I'm flung forward, my forehead banging on the front controls.

Time seems to stand still as I sit there, watching the steam from my breath coil around me, aware of my heart slowing down. Something wet is trickling down my forehead, but when I try to touch it, my right arm, seething with pain, is unable to move. A moaning noise suddenly breaks my concentration, reminding me that Pick is still in the back, badly hurt. I swing the door open with my good arm and poke my head out.

Everyone is running toward me. Lieutenant Andrews, Opal, Cornelia, and about fifty other girls all rush out on the airfield.

"Get a doctor!" I yell at them. "Pick's been injured."

Lieutenant Andrews is the first to the plane. He holds his arm out, helping me climb down. When my feet are on the ground, he grabs me tightly into a hug. "Most people would have jumped, but you risked everything."

Between tears of joy, Cornelia and Opal also each give me a hug. I look over at the plane. Pick is slowly being lowered out and onto a gurney.

"Will he be all right?" I ask the nurse while she straps him down.

"From what I can tell, he hasn't had a concussion. After a few stitches, he'll be good as new. Save for a headache or two. Better let us take a look at your arm and that gash in your forehead." She and one of the other flight instructors wheel him off toward the infirmary.

Cornelia walks up to me. "So what does it feel like to save somebody else's life?"

"I don't know. I saved myself."

"You would have jumped if he weren't in the plane." She pauses a second, looking out at the B-26, as the mechanics push it off of the airfield. "Do you remember our first day of flight training, when I ran my mouth to Pick about not wanting to be your partner?"

"I remember wanting to clobber you more than anything in the world," I answer.

Cornelia smiles. "Pick said something that day. I remember it word for word, because it really angered me. He said that the men overseas would die for each other, and he hasn't met a woman who was able to do the same. He challenged us to prove him wrong. I think you did."

"In a way, Sadie did as well," I answer.

"Well, you obviously passed. Pick better be nice to you from now on. Can you believe this was our last check ride? That there won't be a next time?" Opal remarks.

"You're right. There won't be a next time. But it has nothing to do with the check ride," a voice behind us quivers. We turn around to find Deirdre standing there with a sullen, stunned expression on her face. Her eyes are red with remnants of wetness around the edges. Her shaking fingers grasp a crumpled piece of paper.

As she looks out at the B-26, she cringes and quickly looks away, as if in pain.

"What is it?" I ask. "Is it Leonard? Did you hear something? Did something happen to him?"

"No," she says, tearing up. "It's worse." She holds the paper out toward us.

CHAPTER FOURTEEN

While I was having engine trouble, and everyone on base was out at the airfield waiting for news of my condition, the mail arrived. Deirdre, who had one too many glasses of apple juice at breakfast and could no longer contain herself, ran back to the bay to use the bathroom. That's when she noticed the cream-colored envelops laying on each of our beds. Curious, she opened hers.

—✈—

To Each Member of the WASP:

I am very proud of you young women and the outstanding job you have done as members of the Air Force team. When we needed you, you came through and have served most commendably under very difficult circumstances.

The WASP became part of the Air Forces because we had to explore the nation's total manpower resources in order to release male pilots for other duties. Their very successful record of accomplishment has proved that in any future total effort the nation can count on thousands of its young women to fly any of its aircraft. You have freed male pilots for other work, but now the war situation has changed and the time has come when your volunteered services are no longer needed. The situation is that if you continue in service you will be replacing instead of releasing our young men. I know that the WASP wouldn't want that.

So, I have directed that the WASP program be inactivated and all WASP be released on 20 December, 1944. I want you to know that I appreciate your war service and that the AAF will miss you. I also know that you will join us in being thankful that our combat losses have proven to be much lower than anticipated, even though it meant inactivation of the WASP.

I am sorry that it is impossible to send a personal letter to each of you.

My sincerest thanks and Happy Landings always.

H.H. Arnold
General, U.S. Army
Commanding General, Army Air Forces

By now, a large group of girls has amassed around the wishing well, most with letters in hand.

"I can't believe it. Just like that, they don't need us." Opal crumples her letter up and tosses it in the well.

I stare down, as it sinks beneath the surface of the water, becoming a muddled ball of paper and blurred ink. There's a lump in my throat. "What are we supposed to do now? Just go home? I was really looking forward to going out on assignment. To seeing other parts of the country, and to flying even bigger and better aircraft."

"I was planning to put in a request to be stationed at Love Field in Dallas," Cornelia says, her eyes clouding over with tears. "It would have been close enough for Lowell to be able to drive in on the weekends. Despite the collision with the horrible Mrs. Fairchild at the Governor's Ball, I found Dallas to be surprisingly romantic."

"Dallas was fun, wasn't it?" I smile, remembering every aspect of the dance. The lights. Our dresses. Dancing with Lieutenant Andrews. And then the heartbreaking thought of Sadie wafts through my mind.

"That was the last time John saw Sadie."

Opal looks up. "At least she doesn't have to be here for this. I think she would have taken the news the hardest."

I sit there on the edge of the wishing well, thinking about Sadie and Pa. The thought that it is over is unbearable, and suddenly I feel like I'm about to vomit.

"Byrdie, are you okay?" Opal sits back down next to me.

"It's just…I mean, how do they expect us to…just go home? That's the last place I want to be right now. I miss Mom and Charlotte. I do. But life was so miserable back there."

Cornelia sighs. "You were miserable because you didn't follow your heart."

"I know. And I can't do that anymore. Not after being here. Not after meeting all of you. Not after everything I've accomplished. This is the first time in my life that I've felt alive. It all means too much to just hide it away again."

"I don't even care about the money!" Opal suddenly exclaims. "I'll fly for a dollar. Or for free. They won't have to pay me a cent. Just as long as I can continue to fly the airplanes and help out with the war effort until Daniel gets back."

"Wouldn't matter," Deirdre shakes her head. "There would still be a male pilot out there somewhere who you'd be replacing. Money or no money, that's what it comes down to. The men or us. And unfortunately, there are far more people in authority who would feel safer with a male pilot than a woman in the cockpit. Even though we've proven that our flying abilities are exactly equal."

I look out at the airfield and spot Lieutenant Andrews walking toward the general quarters. I stand up, wiping the dirt off of my zoot suit. "I'll be right back," I tell the others. My left fist clenches the letter as I march hastily out toward the general quarters after him.

As Lieutenant Andrews' hand reaches out for the doorknob of the building, I catch up to him from behind.

"Excuse me, Sir," I exclaim loudly, my lips pressing together with rage.

Lieutenant Andrews stands there a moment, his back to me. He slowly lets go of the doorknob and turns around.

"How long have you known?" I cross my arms.

"Listen, Byrdie—"

"How long?" I ask again.

"A little over a month," he replies, soft-spoken.

I'm taken aback with disgust. I feel as though I've been punched in the gut, and all the wind feels like it's been knocked out of my lungs.

"They told me right before Major Pickett left for D.C. That's why he was there. He was fighting, alongside Jackie, for the program to be militarized instead of deactivated."

"Major Pickett was fighting for us?" I swallow, confused. "I thought he would be happy to see us all leave."

"Major Pickett would never admit it to your faces, but I think he enjoys the challenge of teaching you girls how to fly the Army way and seeing you succeed. Maybe he feels like he's doing the impossible. I'm not sure. He fought hard for you girls, but in the end, they—"

"I know," I say, nodding my head. "They have to do what's best for the country. We don't matter to them. I feel like such a fool." I look out at the airfield, trying as hard as I can to keep the tears in.

"Why? Because you learned to fly the Army way?"

"No," I look him right in the eye. "Because I believed that it would actually matter. And now that I know the truth, to be honest, I wish I had never come at all. Or I wish I had washed out my first week, instead of coming this close to victory only to have it taken away. I don't know what to do with the rest of my life anymore. Everything was planned out just fine. I was supposed to receive my duties, become militarized, perhaps move up in ranking, and enjoy a stable, lifelong career flying for the government. Now I have to start all over again."

"That's not necessarily true. There are other ways." He takes a step toward me. "You're not going to stop flying, Byrdie. I can see it in your eyes. The fire. The desire. It's there. You have a pilot's heart. Just like your father. You'll be just fine."

I feel the tears sliding down my cheeks, down my neck, and onto my zoot suit. Suddenly, Lieutenant Andrews's arms are wrapped around me, holding on tightly, and I am crying against his chest. He pats my back. Strokes my hair. I close my eyes and allow him to comfort me.

For all the prior cadets at Avenger, the night before graduation was an exciting occasion for everyone. Girls would stay up all hours of the night swapping stories, setting each other's hair in curlers, painting their nails bright red, talking about which family members were attending graduation, and making any last minute alterations to the Santiago Blue uniforms that everyone wears during the ceremony.

Not us. Our uniforms hang on the ledge above our window, untouched. I haven't even tried mine on since I got it back from the tailor. It just doesn't seem to matter anymore.

Opal and Deirdre are playing a game of rummy on the other side of the room while I sit on my cot, reminiscing about all of the things that have happened within the walls of this bay over the past six months. Waking up every morning to either the stifling heat or the unbearable cold. Having to fight each other for warm water in the mornings. Rushing to make formation on time. Collapsing onto our cots at the end of long, tiresome days. Staying up to study together the night before our check rides. It all seems to have zipped right by us.

"Where's Cornelia?" Deirdre asks, glancing outside the window. "It's almost lights out."

"She went into town to see a movie with Lowell." I lean forward on my cot. "She said they could give her as many demerits as they please for staying out late. It doesn't matter anymore."

"Wish I had thought of that," Opal says. "We could have made a late movie or gone down to the swimming hole. Instead of being cooped up in here."

"Let's do it!" I suddenly exclaim, the anger and frustration becoming too much for me to tolerate. "Let's just go."

"Right now?" Opal winces as she glances out at the dark night, unsure. "How will we get into town? We can't walk in the dark, and it's far too late to ask someone for a ride."

A sly grin creeps its way across my face. "I happen to know for a fact that Pick's ol' Jeep is parked behind the administrative building, right where he left it before he was injured. And the keys are sitting in the ignition. Since he's been resting these past couple days, he hasn't had any reason to go anywhere. And the administrative building is dead this time of night. Everyone is either in their bay, or in the general quarters on the other side of the base. So what do you both say to a little harmless adventure?"

"I don't know," Opal says, nervously.

"Come on," I answer. "If Sadie were here, she'd be out the door by now. Let's do something crazy for once. Paint the town. We have nothing to lose."

"What about the night watch guard out at the airfield?" Opal asks.

"Who? Earl? He's a softy," I tell her. "Even if he does see us, I'm sure we can talk him into keeping it a secret."

I look at Opal, then at Deirdre. A mischievous glint sparkles in all of our eyes.

We stealthily tiptoe around the back of our bay and gradually make our way behind the long stretch of buildings, toward the mess hall, which is right next to the administrative building. My heart beats rapidly with each crunch of leaves I step on. It's impossible to be quiet when there are leaves everywhere.

"Hey, Byrdie," Deirdre whispers. "You can drive, right?"

I stop in my tracks. They both turn to look at me. "A tractor, maybe," I say with a nod, not liking where this conversation is going. "But not a clunky Jeep like Pick's. What about you?"

She shakes her head. "It's stupid. I'm scared of driving."

"Let me get this straight. You have no problem maneuvering a B-26 bomber, but being behind the controls of a small little Jeep gives you the frights?"

She nods. "I don't like being on the ground. I get claustrophobic. It's not as open as the sky. Last time I tried, I had a panic attack within seconds of placing my hand on the steering wheel."

I sigh and glance over at Opal.

"Don't look at me." She coils back defensively. "I've never driven a day in my life. In New York, we have a wonderful little thing called the bus."

I stand there as Deirdre and Opal both wait for me to say something. I had driven Pa's tractor when I was younger. And the roads were sure to be vacant this time of night. "Okay," I whisper. "If I can master a chandelle, driving should be a cinch. Or at least let's hope that's the case."

Pick's old, tarnished Jeep is parked, just as I predicted, right behind the administrative building. The passenger window is rolled down, and Opal reaches in and unlocks the latch. As quietly as possible, she creaks the door open and climbs up onto the weathered seat. Deirdre follows her, closing the door quietly behind her. Opal leans over and unlocks the driver's door. I slowly pull on the handle and with a rusty squeak, the door opens, and I climb inside.

I stare at the key in the ignition. It almost seems as if it is waiting for me to turn it. I think back to when I used to drive Pa's tractor. I place my foot on the brake, press in the clutch, and slowly turn the key. With a loud rumble, the engine starts. Steam from the warmth of my breath coils around me as I place my hands on the steering wheel at ten and two o'clock, just like Pa taught me.

"You have to move the shifter into first gear with that," Deirdre says, leaning over and gesturing toward the Jeep's clutch.

I take a deep breath and try to shift the car into first gear, but my shoulder seethes with pain. "Opal, you'll need to help me shift gears," I tell her.

Opal leans over and moves us into first and with a huge jolt we lurch forward, heading straight toward a tree.

"Watch out! Hit the brake!" Deirdre screams. I slam my foot down on the brake pedal, causing us to come to a screeching halt.

"Don't yell at me!"

"Sorry!"

"Calm down," Opal says as she puts a hand on each of our shoulders. She turns to Deirdre. "Just give her a moment to get used to driving. She's not used to being on ground." She turns to me. "And you pay attention to where the road is. And no dives or spins."

After a few more tries, I manage to pull the Jeep out from behind the administrative building and toward the dirt road that will take us to town.

It helps that the road is practically vacant. Only one truck passes by us the entire drive. It still causes me to dip into the side of the road, but after it passes, I crawl back into the lane with no problem.

When we reach downtown Sweetwater, we park alongside Main Street, right in front of the soda shop. We pile out, lock up the truck, and I slip the keys into my pocket.

We head in the direction of the movie theater. They're showing *Gaslight* tonight with Ingrid Bergman and Charles Boyer. We've already missed the first forty-five minutes, so we sneak into the dark theater and sit in the back row.

"Do you think it's a good idea that we're here?" Opal whispers in my ear. "What if Cornelia and Lowell want some time alone?"

I look around the room, but I am unable to locate Cornelia's curly blonde silhouette. "I don't think they're here," I whisper back.

Deirdre gasps. "I bet they went to the Bluebonnet Hotel!"

A young couple in front of us turns around and motions for us to be quiet.

"She wouldn't dare go to a hotel with Lowell, would she?" Opal looks at me.

"It's Cornelia. You never know what she's liable to do next." I crane my neck, searching the front rows for any sign of her. "I bet they drove his truck all the way to Mexico and got hitched. That's my guess."

The girl in front of us turns around again, scowling and motioning with her finger for us to be quiet.

"Come on," I whisper, as I stand and sneak back out of the theater.

Opal and Deirdre follow behind.

We tumble out onto the street, erupting in giggles. "We might as well go see if they're at the Bluebonnet, being downtown already and all," Opal suggests. "Besides, aren't you a tad bit curious what it's like inside? After all, we don't have to worry about being caught there anymore."

The Bluebonnet Hotel is off limits to all of the WASP trainees, unless a parent or husband accompanies them. If you want to go have brunch at their dining facilities on the weekends, you have to get a special pass. Occasionally we'd hear rumors of girls sneaking out to meet guys for a drink there in the evenings. After one of them got caught and given enough demerits to confine her to her bay for two months, the rumors stopped.

"I've been dying to see what it's like inside!" Deirdre exclaims, walking ahead of us, toward the building that is only a few blocks away.

"Just for a little while, okay? I want to get the Jeep back before someone notices it's missing."

We approach the hotel, and I remember my first day at Sweetwater. How Sadie and I walked toward these very same steps, and how Cornelia was sitting there, wearing that ridiculous satin dress and fanning herself with a lace hand fan. I remember how horrible she acted toward me, and I laugh the thought out of my head, knowing that person no longer exists.

Deirdre swings the door open. "After you." She motions for us to enter. Opal walks through first. Reluctantly, I follow behind her.

The inside is surprisingly quaint. I envisioned a darkly-lit lounge area with velvet curtains and brass chandeliers. The curtains are white and frilly, and the chandeliers hold real candles.

"Can I help you girls with something?"

We turn around. An older woman eyes us suspiciously from behind a long desk.

"No ma'am, we're just looking for someone," I explain. "Could we glance around the restaurant area for a minute?"

"Gotta buy something," she responds matter-of-factly.

"Do either of you have any money on you?" Deirdre whispers to us. Opal shakes her head. They both look at me.

I sigh. "First I have to drive. Now I have to pay. This is the most poorly-planned adventure I've ever been on. I'm sorry I came up with the idea. Let's go sit down." I push past them and into the dining area.

A few tables are occupied. A couple of male soldiers glance up from a table in the corner. A group of middle-aged women playing bridge look our way. But there's no sign of Cornelia or Lowell.

When we're seated, each of us orders a soda.

"I'm starving!" Deirdre scans over the menu. "Let's get something to eat."

"I only have a few dollars," I remind her.

"A basket of homemade potato chips is only thirty-five cents."

"Fine." I take another sip. "I'm going to run to the ladies' room," I tell the others as I stand and head toward the door marked 'Women' in the corner.

There's someone else in the toilet stall, so I spend a moment staring at my reflection in the mirror. I pull out the bobby pins that hold my hair back and watch as it cascades around my shoulders. Better, I think.

The toilet flushes, and the door behind me opens. I turn around and collide right into my sister Charlotte.

Chapter Fifteen

Time seems to have stopped as Charlotte and I stand there, staring at each other in stunned silence.

"I hardly recognize you," she finally exclaims, catching her breath.

I open my mouth, but nothing comes out.

"Didn't Noah tell you we were coming?" she asks.

I am finally able to regain my tongue. "Y-you mean Lieutenant Andrews?" She nods. "No, he didn't say anything."

"Are you two dating?" She smiles slyly.

"Goodness, no. He's like an older brother to me. Nothing more."

"Mom will be disappointed. She was hoping you were. Apparently he comes from a very nice family. And he's so handsome, Byrdie."

"Mom's here with you?" I ask, not wanting to talk about Lieutenant Andrews any further.

"Of course. She's upstairs trying to rest. The trip was really exhausting for her. Poor thing. As usual, she couldn't get any sleep."

"As usual?" I ask. "What do you mean?"

Charlotte pauses a moment and then folds her arms. "Mom doesn't sleep too well these days."

"Because of me?" I ask, as a lump of guilt forms in the back of my throat. I know that I'm the reason she's not sleeping.

"Oh, Byrdie," Charlotte looks down at the ground. "Stop being so selfish. Can't you for once take a moment to think about someone else beside yourself?"

She looks up at me, and I realize there's something in her eyes that wasn't there before I left. She's older. Her eyes are heavy. Her hair is wiry. Her hands are scuffed. She's struggled. I can see the long hours she spends every day working in the victory garden. I can see her baby-sitting the neighbor's children for mere pennies. I can see her misery.

"Look at you," she says as she looks me over from head to toe. "You're tan and no longer as skinny as a stick. I bet you're having an absolute ball out here, flying your little planes. Just like when you were little. You and Pa would spend hours up there, while Mom and I were left with all the housework. You always get what you want, don't you? Well, I hope you're enjoying it. We can't all be so lucky."

Before I can answer, she opens the door and runs out of the bathroom.

The next morning, December 7, is graduation day. I turn over in bed, my stomach still uneasy from my little run-in with Charlotte. We rise as usual, shower, make our beds, sweep the floors, but instead of our floppy zoot suits, we slip into our new Santiago Blue uniforms, designed by Bergdorf Goodman and fitted by the department store, Neiman Marcus. The uniform consists of a beautifully tailored navy blue skirt and blazer, with a matching beret. We've each been given a pair of nice dress shoes to accompany the uniform.

As Cornelia brushes her hair in front of the bathroom mirror, something peculiar catches my eye.

"Where were you last night?" I walk up behind her.

"Down by Lake Sweetwater. Why?"

"We were looking for you," I respond, and wait a moment before continuing. "What a pretty ring. I've never seen you wear it before. Is it new?"

She stops brushing her hair, and her eyes meet mine in the mirror. Her lips slowly form a shy smile, as she turns around. "Lowell asked me to marry him last night."

Opal stops ironing and Deirdre looks up from tying her shoes.

"I said yes!" Cornelia says, laughing, and her cheeks blush. "The ring isn't fancy," she says, admiring it. "But Lowell made it himself from a scrap of copper. He's an accomplished blacksmith as well as a farm boy."

We all examine it closely, taking turns trying it on our hands.

"We've been saving up our money, so hopefully we'll have enough to put a deposit down on a small house in Capitola. Near his father's farm."

"What about flying?" I ask. "You're not going to stop, are you?"

"Flying was what I used to escape my life in Atlanta, and to be closer to my brother. I'll always love flying, and I'd like to continue it as a hobby. I won't have my own plane, of course. We'll be poor as dirt. Poor but happy." She smiles, thinking about it a moment. "Now, on to more important things. Are you going to let me curl your hair for the ceremony?"

I study my reflection in the mirror. I was planning on wearing it up, but maybe a change would be good. "Okay," I agree, thinking to myself that the more different I look when I see Mom, the better.

The cowbell rings, reminding us that it's time to meet out at the wishing well, as instructed. There are about fifty-eight girls in our class graduating today. We stand out by the well and toss coins into it for good luck, watching them fall along the rocky bottom, until we are instructed to line up in pairs of two.

The graduation is being held out at the flight line. As we march in twos, past our bays, the administrative building, the mess hall, I wonder what will become of Avenger Field after we leave. Will the men move back in the day after we're deactivated? It's a sad thought. I shake it out of my head and try to pay attention to the ceremony.

Because we're the last class to graduate at Avenger, about a hundred or so upperclassmen have shown up to support us. They sit in their service uniforms on the side and as we pass by, they clap loudly.

We march to the front of the field, to the rows of chairs that have been set out for us. We sit down one at a time. In front of us is a platform, where Jackie Cochran, Hap Arnold, and a few other high-ranking officials from Washington, D.C. sit before us.

A trumpet is playing "Hymn to Avenger," and everyone sings along with it.

In the land of crimson sunsets,
Skies are wide and blue,
Stands a school of many virtues,
Loved by old and new.

'Neath Old Glory's banners waving
We fly from dawn till dusk,
In God's hand our futures tarry,
And in Him we trust.

Gone before are many daughters,
To carry on her name,
May we live in faith and honor,
Yet to bring her fame.

Long before our duty's ended,
A mem'ry you shall be,
In our hearts we pledge devotion,
Avenger Field to thee!

When we are done, a hush falls over the crowd as Jackie Cochran rises and walks toward the podium.

"It seems incredible," she starts, "that you can have so many different emotions. Happiness. Sorrow. Pride. I have all three of those today. I'm very happy that we've trained a thousand women to fly the Army way. I think it's going to mean more to aviation than anyone realizes. I'm very happy that General Arnold, who made this possible, is here for the final phase of this wonderful program—this program that will go down in history. I'm sure it's going to do something that is so vital, and that is to heighten the awareness of women's interest in flying for their country."

The crowd applauds. Jackie puts her arms in the air to silence everyone. "And I'm sure that if there's a reason to call you girls back up after December 20, that all of you will respond and that we'll have probably ninety-five percent of you back in the Air Forces. And now it is my pleasure to introduce you all to General Hap Arnold, Commanding General of the Army Air Forces."

The crowd applauds as General Arnold rises from his seat and walks toward the podium. He is wearing his entire uniform, with countless patches and insignias all over his olive-colored shirt and blazer. I can hardly believe that the general of the entire Air Force is standing in front of us. He smiles warmly as his hand reaches for the microphone.

"I am glad to be here today to talk with you young women who have been making aviation history. You and all WASP have been pioneers in a new field of wartime service, and I sincerely appreciate the splendid job you have done for the AAF. You, and more than nine hundred of your sisters, have shown that you can fly wingtip to wingtip with your brothers. If there was ever a doubt in anyone's mind that women can become skillful pilots, the WASP have dispelled that doubt.

"The possibility of using women to pilot military aircraft was first considered in the summer of 1941. We anticipated then that global war would require all our qualified men and many of our women. England and Russia had already instructed women to fly trainers and combat-type aircraft, and Russian women were being used in combat.

"I called in the most accomplished female pilot in the country, Jacqueline Cochran, who had herself flown almost everything with wings and several times had won air races from men who are now general officers of the Air Forces. I asked her to draw a plan for the training and use of American women pilots. She presented such a plan in late 1941, and it formed the basis for the Air Force's use of WASP.

"My objectives in forming the WASP were three things. First, to see if women could serve as military pilots, and if so, to form the nucleus of an organization which could be rapidly expanded. Second, to release male pilots for combat. And third, to decrease the Air Force's total demands for the cream of the manpower pool.

"Well now, in 1944, more than two years since WASP first started flying with the Air Forces, we can come to only one conclusion: The entire operation has been a success. It is on record that women can fly as well as men. Certainly, we haven't been able to build an airplane you can't handle. From AT-6s to B-29s, you have flown them around like veterans. One of the WASP has even test-flown our new jet plane.

"We are winning the war. We still have a long way to go, but we are winning it. Every WASP who has contributed to the training and operation of the Air Force has filled a vital and necessary place in the jigsaw pattern of victory. Some of you are discouraged at times—all of us are—but be assured you have filled a necessary place in the overall picture of the U.S. Air Forces.

"The WASP have completed their mission. Their job has been successful. But, as is usual in war, it has not been without cost. Thirty-eight WASP have died while helping their country move toward the moment of final victory. The Air Forces will long remember their service and their final sacrifice.

"So on this last graduation day, I salute you and all WASP. We of the AAF are proud of you. We will never forget our debt to you."

The airfield erupts into applause as General Arnold raises his hand to his head, saluting us. He then returns to his seat.

Our entire class stands up, and we are called up to the stage one at a time to receive our wings.

"I'm so nervous," Opal mutters to me. "I hope I don't fall flat on my face."

"You'll do fine," I tell her, as they call her name and she walks up the steps where Jackie stands. She pins Opal's wings on, shakes her hand, and Opal walks off the stage.

"Bernadette Thompson."

I take a deep breath, walk up the steps, and stand in front of Jackie, who is cradling my shiny pair of wings in her hand.

"I knew you'd make it," she whispers as she pins the wings on the left side of my blazer. "See? Even a poor farm girl from Iowa can make a difference if she tries hard enough." She shakes my hand, and I can't even describe the feeling. It's as though a surge of electricity has flooded through every bone, every nerve, and every muscle of my body. I feel truly alive as I walk off the platform and return to my seat.

I look over to the side. Mom and Charlotte are sitting among all the other girls' family members. Mom catches my eye. We stare at each other for a long moment. Next to her, Charlotte scowls down at me, her arms folded across her chest. I quickly look away, my heart suddenly beating rapidly.

I turn and look out at the airfield. The sun shines brightly, turning the clouds that float along the stretch of blue sky a wonderful shade of peach. A hazy film wafts up from the flat red dirt, and I swear someone—a man, my father—is standing at the horizon, watching me.

I turn back to the podium to see Cornelia receive her wings, but when I look back out at the horizon, he is gone.

After the ceremony is over, we stand together on the airfield, taking countless class photos.

Cornelia leans over toward me. "My parents are furious about Lowell."

"You told them?"

"May as well get it out in the open while everyone's here, right? Anyway, Father is outside pacing angrily by the Rolls Royce at the moment, debating whether or not to leave early, and Mother fainted when she heard the news."

"Where's Lowell?"

"At the infirmary, with Mother. He's determined to win her over with his Texas charm. Your family's here, right?"

I sigh. "Lieutenant Andrews took it upon himself to invite them for me. Gave them money to stay at the Bluebonnet and everything."

"You don't seem pleased about it."

"I just don't really know what to say to them anymore. My sister's mad at me, and I'm starting to realize that my being here was harder on my mother than I had thought. And I don't know what they'll say when I tell them I'm going to keep flying. I wish Sadie was here. She always had all the answers."

Cornelia puts her arm around my shoulder as the bulbs from the camera keep flashing at us.

When the pictures are over, I roam around the field, trying to avoid having to speak with Mother and Charlotte, who are in the mess hall at the reception.

I sit down on one of the graduation chairs and gaze out at the airplanes lined up in the distance, gleaming in the sunlight.

"So what's next for Byrd Thompson?" a voice bellows behind me. I turn around. Jackie Cochran stands beside me, her arms crossed against her chest.

"I don't know," I tell her. "I'm still figuring that out. It's hard knowing this is over and I have to decide what to do next."

She laughs and sits down next to me. "You'll be fine," she tells me. "The hard part's already over. You can fly pursuits, trainers, and bombers. You studied meteorology, Morse code, flight theory, and engines. Speaking of which, you also landed a plane without engine power!"

"You heard about that?"

"Major Pickett would never admit it, but he was very pleased with your flying. He said you had the most potential of any of the girls in his class. Because you had the most to learn initially, but exceeded everyone's expectations."

"I thought he hated women pilots."

"So he claims," Jackie says. "But I have a feeling it's only because he knows we're just as good as the men. Major Pickett was right beside me in Washington fighting for the program. Don't let it discourage you. The government doesn't own the sky. It's still yours, if you want it. Now come on and join the others in the mess hall. This is a day of celebration!"

Mom and Charlotte are standing on the side of the room. I make my way over to them, hugging and patting several of my classmates on the back along the way. My stomach churns with nervous uncertainty as I approach them.

Charlotte is eating a piece of cake, and I realize that it's probably been years since she had frosting made with real butter and cream. I look up at Mom and notice that her hair is grayer than it was before I left. A few new wrinkles spread across her forehead. Her face is paler than I remember it being.

"Hi, Mom." I shift from side to side, uncomfortably.

She stares at me a moment and then crosses her arms. Her teeth clench. "Do you have any idea how painful it was to wake up that morning and find a note on the kitchen table explaining how my youngest daughter has left home for another state without saying goodbye?"

"I'm sorry, but I had to go." I press my lips together, trying to suppress the guilt that's filling every inch of me.

"You could have told me in person. I would have liked to say goodbye properly. That was the worst thing you've ever done to me. Do you realize that every minute of every day I have been tortured with the thought that if something were to happen to you, I never would have the chance to say goodbye? Did you ever think about that?"

"No," I answer, suddenly ashamed of myself. "I'm sorry. I was scared."

"So was I. I was scared that I'd lose another—" Her words trail off as she turns toward Charlotte, who wraps her arms around her, comforting her.

"For six months she's been like this," Charlotte says, glaring at me. "And it's all your fault."

I want to run. I want to fling open the door of the administrative building and sprint out to the airfield. I want to jump into an AT-11, take off, and spend the rest of my life in the sky.

"Mom," I place my hand on the back of her shoulder. "I never did any of this to hurt or upset you. I fly because it gives me pleasure and a purpose in life. It makes me happy. Is that so wrong? To want to be happy?"

Charlotte turns toward me. "Happy?" She snorts. "Pa was happy, and look what happened to him."

"You've always blamed me for his death," I say as I stare at her. "That's why I'm here. I blamed myself as well. I needed to know what went wrong. I wanted to know if there was anything I could have done. Listen, I know that I'm taking risks. That it's dangerous to some degree."

"To some degree?" Mom turns away from Charlotte and looks

at me again. "I read in the papers how one of the young girls in your class crashed and died. Why put yourself in that kind of danger? It's stupid."

"I knew that girl." I suppress the tears as the memory of that day comes back to me. "Very well, in fact. And I also know that if she could go back and do it differently, she wouldn't change a thing." I pause a moment. "And neither would Pa."

"Your father flew to put bread on the table. He didn't have a choice. You have your whole life ahead of you. There's more to life than flying." Her voice becomes angry, and I glance around to make sure nobody is listening to us. I notice Lieutenant Andrews standing across the room, chatting with one of the other trainee's parents. And that's when it dawns on me.

"Come on, Mom," I say, grabbing her arm.

"Where are we going?" she asks, looking down at my hand in alarm.

"There's something I need you to do for me. And for yourself."

"I can't believe you're making me do this," Mom says as I tighten the flight goggles over her eyes. "I wish they weren't all watching."

As soon as everyone heard I was taking a plane up, they all ran out to the airfield to watch.

I wait as Lieutenant Andrews brings a PT-19A around to the flight line.

"I can't," Mom says, shaking her head, turning around. "I can't do this."

"It's the only way you'll ever understand me," I tell her. "I need you to. If we get up there and you hate it, we'll come back down right away. I promise."

Lieutenant Andrews climbs down out of the plane and walks toward us. "Ready for takeoff?"

Mom looks up at him, fear and hesitation all over her face.

"Now, Mrs. Thompson, there's absolutely nothing to be scared of,"

Lieutenant Andrews assures her. "You're daughter's an ace pilot. You're in good hands."

"Did you inspect the plane?" Mom asks.

"Three times thoroughly," he replies.

Mom nods, looking over at me, then at the crowd. "Oh, let's get this over with. Our train leaves in a couple of hours."

I check form one. Set the breaks. Flap up and adjust the rudder to three degrees and wait until the oil pressure is up to fifty pounds, gear the engine up, then tenderly prop forward.

I can almost feel Mom's heart beating in the seat behind me as we gain speed down the flight line. When we're moving fast enough, I slowly pull back on the stick, and the wheels lift up off the ground. We become weightless.

I look over the side at the crowd below. They all strain their necks as they watch us ascend. I turn the plane lightly to the left, away from them, and gain a little speed as we fly toward the West Texas farmland.

When we're at a high enough altitude, I center the stick into a smooth cruising position, and we float.

Any minute now I expect Mom to grab my chair. To demand that we go back immediately. But as we fly together with the clouds to our right, and the sunset to our left, she says absolutely nothing.

I finally get up enough courage to look at her in the rearview mirror. She is gazing out at the sunset, the wind rippling through her hair and against her face.

"I had forgotten," she says, sensing my gaze. "I had forgotten what it feels like to be up here."

She turns and our eyes meet in the mirror. Tears stream down her cheeks, but she is smiling.

"Thank you for reminding me," she says with an air of peace about her that I haven't seen in many, many years.

"Oh, I haven't had that much fun in a long while," Mom exclaims as I help her down from the plane. When I turn to face the crowd, I am surprised to see Cornelia and Charlotte standing together out in front. But what baffles me the most is that Charlotte is wearing Cornelia's zoot suit. I walk toward them.

"What's this about?" I ask, looking at Cornelia and then at Charlotte.

"Take me up there," Charlotte says, her lips pursing together with determination. "When I was little I never understood what all the fuss was about flying."

I look at Cornelia, who flashes her familiar smile that I have grown to adore. "From one sister to another," she says, and then turns, joining Lowell in the sea of people.

"Alright," I tell Charlotte. "But first we have to go through some basic procedures." She nods. "And no screaming like you did when you were little."

"I was ten!" she exclaims. "Pa kept flipping the plane around. I nearly vomited."

"Nearly?" I arch an eyebrow. "I remember one time you got so sick that you—"

"Now, Byrd." She smiles, throwing her head back with laughter and swinging her arm around my shoulder. "Let's put the past behind us, okay?"

CHAPTER SIXTEEN

Even though we've graduated already, we're required to stay on base another twelve days until deactivation. Since we've completed all our training, there really isn't much to do. Already they're starting to send many of our beloved planes to bases elsewhere in the country, wherever there is a shortage. It's a sad sight to see, and we try to spend as much time as possible away from the airfield.

One afternoon I'm lounging around the bay and the mail arrives. I go through the bundle, letter by letter, when something catches my eye. I look up at Deirdre.

"Where's Opal?" I ask.

"I think in the rec room, playing ping-pong. Why?"

"There's a letter here for her, from New York."

"Is it her mother?"

"No, this handwriting is in English. It looks like Daniel's."

"But he's not in New York. He's still overseas."

"I know. It's strange."

We head over to the rec room, where Opal is beating one of our classmates in a game of ping-pong.

"Hey Opal, the mail came." I sit down near the table.

"Not now," she exclaims. "I'm creaming her."

I take a deep breath. "Something came for you from New York."

Opal misses the ball and turns toward me. I pull the letter out of my pocket, and hand it to her.

It takes her only a split second to recognize the handwriting. "It's from Daniel." Without delay, she tears it open and rapidly begins to read.

"Oh, my goodness." She grabs her heart, becoming light-headed, and falls down on the bench next to me.

"Is he okay?" I put my arm on her shoulder.

"He was hurt overseas and has been in a hospital for the past month. During an air raid, he was hit by the gunfire from an overhead aircraft. And…" She chokes up. "He lost a leg."

She sits there, numb.

"It could have been much worse," I whisper.

"Leg or no leg, at least he's alive, and you know where he is," Deirdre says as she sits down on the other side. "I still have no word about Leonard's condition or whether negotiations for prisoners have begun at all. The news says so little about those kinds of things."

Cornelia walks into the room, four bottles of soda crammed in her arms. "There you girls are," she says as she walks over to us. She sits down next to me and hands us each a bottle.

"What's the occasion?" I ask.

"No occasion." She notices Opal's tear-stained face. "Opal, what's wrong?"

"It's Daniel. He was hurt overseas."

"Oh, my gosh. What happened? Is he okay? Wait. Before you tell me, Byrdie, Lieutenant Andrews is looking for you. He wants you to meet him out in the hangar."

"What does he want?"

She shrugs. "Heck if I know. Seemed important."

As I approach the hanger, I see him leaning against an AT-6, arms crossed, waiting for me.

"Hello." He uncrosses his arms and takes a step toward me.

I cross my arms and look up at him. "You wanted to see me?"

He looks down at me with a look of sorrow that I know can only mean one thing. "You're leaving, aren't you?" I ask.

He nods. "Tomorrow morning. I received orders to report for my new duties."

"I see." I knew this moment was coming, but it clutched at my chest in a way I hadn't expected it to.

He looks out at the airfield. "But before I report for my new duties I am to transport five AT-6s from Avenger to a base out in San Diego. Unfortunately, I don't have enough time to fly back and forth myself, so I'll need four top pilots to take on these duties with me. So what do you say?"

"Me?"

"You, Cornelia, Opal, and Deirdre. Well, depending on whether everyone wants to or not. It's not a requirement. I just thought you all could use at least one cross-country assignment before going home."

"Of course they'll want to!" I exclaim. "We've all been going nuts having nothing to do and watching all the planes leave." I smile, a wave of excitement crashing over me as I stare out at the AT-6s.

"There's something else," Lieutenant Andrews says, and I look back up at him. "My new orders are to instruct a group of men out at a base in Cedar Rapids."

"In Iowa?" I immediately ask, my heart skipping a beat with nervous delight as he nods.

"You know I'd offer you a job in a second if I was allowed to," he says, staring uncomfortably at the ground.

I nod, the pain of not being able to fly for my country causing a lump in the back of my throat.

"But I do have a good friend who lives outside Des Moines," he continues. "He owns a civilian base. He's getting older, and his arthritis is acting up. He's looking to hire another instructor any day now, and I'm going to recommend you. That is, if you're interested."

Time seems to stop as I stand there, in complete shock. An instructor? Me? Just like Pa.

"So what do you say?" he asks, but before I realize what I'm doing my arms are around him, hugging him closely.

"Of course I'm interested," I tell him, breaking away.

"Well, then. Good. I think you'd make a fantastic instructor. And Cedar Rapids isn't that far of a drive. I could come up on the weekends to see how things are going."

"Still watching over me?" I ask coyly, tossing my head to one side.

"No," he replies, smiling down at me, his blue eyes gazing into mine. "Just watching you."

The next morning, we wake up at the crack of dawn, shower, and change into our zoot suits. We're ecstatic about leaving Texas and getting to fly across New Mexico, Arizona, Nevada, and finally on into California.

Lieutenant Andrews meets us all out on the flight line at six o'clock, and together we go over various maps of the route we are taking.

We suit up into our parachute packs, and together the five of us walk toward the shimmering AT-6s that are lined up next to each other, as if they have been waiting for us all night. One at a time, we jump into the cockpits and adjust our goggles and helmets.

"All clear!" Lieutenant Andrews yells at us from his plane. "Byrdie, take her on up."

"Me? First?" I holler back.

"Yep. Lead the way!"

I unlock the controls. Set the parking brakes. Flap up. Set the rudder to three degrees. Trim the tab to zero. Crack the throttle three-fourths of the way and check the instruments. I am ready for takeoff, and I prop forward.

I am roaring down the flight line, and with a pull of the stick I begin to ascend, slow and steady. I switch to the fuller tank of gas, crank the flaps up, and circle around once until I'm on target with our course of flight.

Heading northwest, I glance out the window. Cornelia and Opal have already taken off and are trailing behind me, each on one side, forming a "V" shape in the air. In a few moments Deirdre and Lieutenant Andrews will be following behind them. I feel like a mother goose, leading her flock to a warmer climate for the winter.

In front of me, the vast, limitless sky is illuminated by rich purples and quiet yellows that swirl together, hitting the Texas red dirt at the edge of the world.

I know this moment won't last. That this sunrise is fleeing with every ray of light the sun emits, as it climbs higher into the sky. Soaring around in the air, I am aware that the world is constantly in motion below me. And that life is constantly shifting around me. The present is slowly slipping away, second by second. And the past is farther away than we want it to be. But the future is closer than we think.

I can see it, rising up over the horizon in the distance. The future. A mysterious, untried landscape that stretches out in front of us. And for once in my life, I'm not scared of the unknown. Quite the opposite. It excites me.

With a quick push of the stick, I rapidly gain speed, as the clouds dart by my window and become elements of the past. My past. With thrilling uncertainty, I steer toward the unwritten history that stretches out before me like a scroll of blank paper. I plan to write on it, using a confident pen to carve my own path and discover my own meaning.

Maybe all I needed to learn first was how to operate the controls.

The End

AFTERWORD

The WASP were deactivated on December 20, 1944. They packed their bags, said goodbye to each other, and paid for their own tickets home. They held no veteran status, didn't receive any benefits, and became lost in the pages of history.

In 1975, Colonel Bruce Arnold, the son of General Hap Arnold, recognized this injustice and helped the remaining WASP fight to obtain recognition of their contribution to the allied victory in WWII. Together they distributed petitions, lobbied their representatives in Washington, D.C., wrote letters, attended hearings, and tried to make the country aware that women had flown in WWII.

Hearing their voices, on November 23, 1977, President Jimmy Carter signed into legislation a bill granting veteran status to the Women Airforce Service Pilots.

There are less than 600 WASP still alive today, and their numbers are increasingly slipping. Despite their military status, historians writing official history textbooks do not record their contribution.

It is up to us to learn about and share their story with others. It is my hope, in writing this book, that I have done just that.

DATE DUE

DE 17 '09			

FOLLETT